SPECIAL MESSAGE TO READERS

THE ULVERSCROFT FOUNDATION
(registered UK charity number 264873)

was established in 1972 to provide funds for research, diagnosis and treatment of eye diseases. Examples of major projects funded by the Ulverscroft Foundation are:-

- The Children's Eye Unit at Moorfields Eye Hospital, London
- The Ulverscroft Children's Eye Unit at Great Ormond Street Hospital for Sick Children
- Funding research into eye diseases and treatment at the Department of Ophthalmology, University of Leicester
- The Ulverscroft Vision Research Group, Institute of Child Health
- Twin operating theatres at the Western Ophthalmic Hospital, London
- The Chair of Ophthalmology at the Royal Australian College of Ophthalmologists

You can help further the work of the Foundation by making a donation or leaving a legacy. Every contribution is gratefully received. If you would like to help support the Foundation or require further information, please contact:

THE ULVERSCROFT FOUNDATION
The Green, Bradgate Road, Anstey
Leicester LE7 7FU, England
Tel: (0116) 236 4325

website: www.foundation.ulverscroft.com

BRIEF ECSTASY

Rosemary takes a job in Spain, as a companion to Mercedes. Then, on the brief few hours train journey to Malaga, Rosemary meets Paul and falls completely under his spell. But her dreams of love are shattered when she meets Mercedes, and learns of her engagement to Paul. Hurt and angry, Rosemary hatches a devious plan. Heavily veiled, she changes places with the bride at Mercedes' wedding to Paul — but the consequences are quite different to how she had imagined . . .

DENISE ROBINS

BRIEF ECSTASY

Complete and Unabridged

LINFORD
Leicester

First published in Great Britain in 1934

First Linford Edition
published 2013

British Library CIP Data

Robins, Denise, *1897 – 1985.*
    Brief ecstasy. - -
    (Linford romance library)
    1. Love stories.
    2. Large type books.
    I. Title II. Series
    823.9′12–dc23

ISBN 978–1–4448–1507–8

Published by
F. A. Thorpe (Publishing)
Anstey, Leicestershire

Set by Words & Graphics Ltd.
Anstey, Leicestershire
Printed and bound in Great Britain by
T. J. International Ltd., Padstow, Cornwall

This book is printed on acid-free paper

1

'What are you doing for this year's holiday, Rosemary?'

Rosemary Wallace, filing letters as the final effort of work before the end of office hours, looked over her shoulder at the woman who had just put the question to her. Ida Bryant, dear old Ida, who was confidential secretary to the head of the firm, and chief of the staff here. Ida, plain of face, with her horn-rims and lanky hair which she wore in a bun and refused to bob, but who had a romantic heart and the most generous of natures under that unattractive exterior. She was Rosemary's best friend, and of course Ida had adored Rosemary from the time she first came to Tring & Sons as a typist, two years ago. Rosemary, as flower-like and fragrant as her name, and as young and slim and lovely as

Ida was the reverse.

Last year Ida had taken her usual lonely holiday in the Devon hamlet which was her paradise. She had wanted Rosemary with her, but Rosemary's mother was alive and she had had to go away with her. But this year Rosemary was alone in the world, Mrs. Wallace having died, soon after Christmas, of double-pneumonia.

Rosemary still lived in the little flat in Hampstead which had been her home for as long as she could remember, but Miss Bryant was always hoping Rosemary would join up with her. Indeed Rosemary had promised to do so as soon as she could dispose of the lease of the flat.

'My dear Ida,' Rosemary answered her friend, 'it's a bit early in the year to talk of holidays.'

Ida Bryant looked out of the office window. Through a veil of dust she could see a pale orange glow . . . sunset over the river. And all day long she had seen the sun, and it had made her remember that this was April and that spring was at hand.

'Summer will be on us before we know where we are,' she sighed.

'Well, I don't know what I'm going to do,' said Rosemary.

'Come down to Devon with me.'

'Maybe I will, but you know I want . . . '

Rosemary stopped and bit her lip. The older woman continued for her:

'Oh, yes, I know. You want to go abroad. You're hankering after Spain. You're Spain-mad, my dear. Ever since you started taking Spanish at those night classes and saw that Spanish film with me.'

Rosemary walked to her desk, sat down, took a little mirror and a powder-puff from her bag, and dusted a small and attractive nose. It was an altogether very attractive young face which smiled a trifle wistfully at her from the mirror. And with the delicacy of feature, the fragility which the transparent skin and fair, almost ash-gold hair suggested, was

3

fire and spirit. Rosemary at heart was a passionate and impetuous person who hated the routine office life — the whole grey, dreary confinement of the existence which she had been forced to lead since she left school. Nobody looking at Rosemary's curved red mouth with the almost impatient curl of the short upper lip, or into the warm, hazel-gold of her eyes, would deem her as placid, as tranquil as her name suggested.

Ida Bryant, who knew her, realised this fact with some trepidation. She often wondered what would happen to Rosemary Wallace . . . particularly when some young man as attractive and impetuous as herself came along. She only hoped Rosemary would find the right person. At the present moment there was nobody. Rosemary was not interested in any of the men she met through her work — and little wonder, thought Ida Bryant. They were none of them worth looking at twice.

But why this craze for Spain and things Spanish? Miss Bryant, a solid

Britisher and very Conservative, mistrusted all foreigners, and had never once wanted to go out of her own country for a holiday.

She thought Rosemary crazy to study Spanish so arduously. Although she had to admit that the girl was not wasting her time. Already she could speak with surprising fluency and even read a Spanish novel. Miss Bryant regarded this with awe but secret misgiving.

'Rosemary Wallace, you're not thinking of going to Spain for your holiday, are you?' she asked, eyeing her over the rim of her spectacles.

'There's nothing I'd like better,' said Rosemary. 'And if only I could afford it . . . but I don't suppose I can. Ida, darling, you don't know how Spain attracts me. The more I know of the language, the more I like it.'

'Poof, my dear. A nasty, dirty uncivilised place full of barbarians. It was bad enough when they had an English queen on the throne, but now they've turned her and the king out of the country I'm sure it's not a fit place to live in. You'd get shot by a revolutionary as soon as you ever entered Madrid.'

Rosemary went into peals of laughter.

'Ida, darling, you are killing!'

'Well, the papers are always talking of revolution and bloodshed.'

'There's political trouble in the country, I know. But I've met heaps of people at the classes who have been to Spain and had glorious holidays. And one or two Spanish students who laugh at the reports in the papers. They're always exaggerated.'

'Then are you seriously contemplating . . . ?'

'Not so much a holiday as a job.' And now Rosemary Wallace blurted out a secret she had meant to keep, but which excited her so that she had to reveal it: 'Ida, darling, as a matter of fact I've been answering advertisements, and I'm in touch with a lady in Spain who wants an English companion for her daughter. It had to be somebody who could speak the language, and I managed to write quite a nice little letter in Spanish and it was very well received. In fact, I am to interview the sister in London to-morrow, Saturday, afternoon. And, if I please her, I'm going to throw up my job here and go out to Spain at the end of the month.'

Miss Bryant received this news in stony silence — just staring at her young friend over the rim of her glasses. She was used to disappointments. Life had never been very kind to her. But this seemed the unkindest blow of all — to remove from her path this fair, attractive girl, who was not only a delightful person to work with, but a fresh, sweet companion outside the office. All the starved mother-love in Ida Bryant's heart had been given to Rosemary Wallace since their first meeting. She could hardly bear to contemplate losing her so completely . . . losing her to a job which would take her right out of England. And to that country which Ida doggedly believed was barbaric and where a lot of dark wolves would probably swallow her darling lamb up completely.

Rosemary walked over to the desk at which her friend was sitting, slightly bowed, and put an arm around the shrunken figure in the cheap skirt and knitted jumper.

'Darling, is it an awful shock to you? I didn't tell you before because I wanted to be sure I was going to get the job, and I'm almost certain now . . . that is, unless the Spanish lady takes a violent dislike to me when she sees me.'

'It certainly is a shock,' said the older woman slowly. 'And it isn't as though I don't want you to better yourself, or that I recommend anybody to spend a lifetime, as I've done, in this God-forsaken office. But I don't like the idea of losing you, Rosemary, and that's certain!'

'I shall miss you too. You've been terribly good to me.'

'And now you'll go to your beloved

Spain and forget all about me.'

'Certainly I won't. I shall never forget you, Ida. There's no reason why we shouldn't go on being friends. I'll write to you, heaps. And I don't suppose my job will last for long. Maybe less than a year. I believe this girl, to whom I'm to be companion, is half-engaged now, although she is only eighteen. And when she's married I'll come back.'

'Or get another job in Spain,' said Miss Bryant gloomily.

Rosemary gave a little sigh. She stretched her arms above her head with unconscious grace, and the older woman looked at her graceful figure and felt a pang of apprehension. She was so pretty, Rosemary. Those nasty, swarthy Spaniards would all fall in love with her, and who would she have to look after her.

'I only wish it wasn't Spain!' she exclaimed. 'I'd rather you were going anywhere but abroad like this.'

'Oh, but that's the whole thrill of it . . . the fact that it's taking me abroad, and especially to Spain.'

'Well, I suppose you know best.'

'It's what I've worked for,' said Rosemary. 'I've absolutely slaved at my Spanish all this last year.'

'Oh, well, I must accustom myself to it,' said Ida Bryant. 'But I'm going to miss you horribly.'

And she took off her glasses and wiped them, blinking.

Rosemary tried to cheer her up. She, herself, had no desire to break up what had been a very close friendship. But the thrill of adventure was in her veins, and it was queer how the thought of Spain fascinated her. She liked anything that was Spanish ... dances, music, castanets; the high combs and lace mantillas that she saw in pictures, shawls; paintings which showed white courtyards and balconies, orange and lemon trees, flowers and sunlight drenching everything. The very word Spain breathed romance to her. And the more she studied the language and books on the country, the more deeply she became absorbed.

Now nothing would content her but to go to Spain, and this seemed her big chance.

Riding on a bus through the London twilight that evening toward the inexpensive *brasserie* where they were to have supper together, Rosemary tried to interest Ida Bryant on the subject, gave her more details about the impending job.

To-morrow she was going to the Cumberland Hotel to meet this Spanish lady whose sister, Señora Lamanda, had advertised for an English companion for her daughter, Mercedes.

The Lamandas, so Rosemary had learned, through a Spanish student, at the night classes, were a very powerful and well-known family in Spain. They were enormously wealthy, and had not had their estates or wealth removed from them, like so many royalists, because they were 'in' with the present Government.

'In the letter that I received from

Señora Lamanda,' Rosemary told Ida, 'she said that they lived partly in Madrid and partly in Malaga, where they have a villa, some seven or eight miles out of the town. I am to go to this villa and spend the next few months giving English lessons to Mercedes and accompanying her wherever they go.'

'Well, it all sounds very interesting,' Miss Bryant was forced to agree, 'but I don't like it.'

'Don't like what?'

'The thought of you in Spain.'

'But what on earth can happen to me? I shall have a marvellous time with people who have so much money and influence.'

'If you marry a Spaniard I'll never forgive you.'

Rosemary's golden eyes danced.

'Old idiot; why should I? There's no question of me going out there and getting married. I'm going to a job.'

'And will this sister take you out there?'

'No. She's over for the summer. I'm

going out alone.'

Miss Bryant's face grew longer.

'So you're going to travel alone? I don't like it.'

'Well I shall like it,' said Rosemary laughing. 'It will all be a most thrilling adventure. But don't let's either of us get too het up over it. Señora Lamanda's sister may take a violent dislike to me and refuse to engage me.'

'I'm afraid there's no chance of that,' said Ida.

And of course she was right. Twenty-four hours later Rosemary's fate was sealed. The interview with the Spanish lady at the Cumberland Hotel had proved entirely satisfactory. Rosemary's good looks and charming manners had won the day for her, and she on her part had thought the Señora charming. If the Lamandas were like that, everything would be perfect. The Señora had even had a photograph of her niece to show Rosemary, and that had thrilled her. Mercedes Lamanda, at eighteen, wearing a high comb and white lace mantilla, looked ravishingly lovely. And a glowing description of the Villa Santa Barbara, near Malaga, fired Rosemary's imagination. It all just sounded too good to be true. Her most cherished dreams were going to be realised. It was impossible for Rosemary to regret answering the advertisement and taking the job.

It only remained for her to give in her notice at the office and settle up affairs at home and she could be off. Off to Spain, to the sunlight, the romance, for which she had worked and about which she had dreamed for so long. Perhaps the one regret was Ida . . . poor old Ida, who was so fond of her and relied so on her company. But life was like that. There had to be a wrench of some kind, and after all the job might not last long and she would come back and be with Ida again. Now that she was so fluent at her Spanish, she felt that she would always get work of some kind — in London if not abroad.

Ida was a stand-by until the last; helped her let the flat, and dispose of her furniture, and spend some of the money that her mother had left her on an outfit. It was early spring in London, but in Malaga it would be like summer. The Señora had told her to take thin frocks. There would be bathing and tennis and picnics in the mountains, and all the delightful recreations of summer in full swing.

Little wonder that Rosemary was thrilled when she bought and packed a variety of silky summer dresses, a pair of gay beach pyjamas, a big hat or two, and some evening dresses . . . the first really smart ones she had ever possessed, because never before had she been so extravagant. With her hair properly set, and her nails manicured, she tried on the new clothes, and found herself transformed. And Ida looked at the lovely, elegant young figure, and felt that she had indeed lost the little Rosemary of office days.

Nevertheless, despite her reluctance to part from Rosemary and her mistrust of Spain and this adventure, she tried not to cast a shadow over Rosemary's happiness, and kept her doubts to herself.

Then came the day when Miss Bryant got the morning away from the office in order to see her young friend off to Spain. A thrilling morning for Rosemary, and a sad one for the elder woman, tinged with anxiety. She kept feeling that something might happen to Rosemary . . . something she did not bargain for. And she could not help telling her so at the last moment, when they were standing on the platform at Victoria just before the boat train left for Dover.

Rosemary patted her back and laughed at her, as usual.

'Silly old darling; what on earth can happen to me?'

'Oh, you never know, in a strange foreign country; and after all these Lamandas are completely unknown to you and different from any of your own countrymen.'

'Dear old Ida, you're thoroughly prejudiced,' Rosemary murmured. 'But it will be perfectly all right, I assure you.'

'Well, you will write to me often and tell me everything won't you?'

'I'll give you my word on that.'

Miss Bryant gave a last fond look at her friend. There was pride as well as love in her tired eyes. Rosemary looked marvellous in that travelling suit of light blue and grey summer tweed, with an organdie blouse, and long blue-grey tweed coat with a high collar; belt around the slender waist, and a blue beret at rakish angle on the fair head to complete a very attractive outfit. The blue leather bag, with her monogram in silver, was Ida's parting present to her. And she was travelling with a new dressing-bag and an old but still good cabin trunk which had belonged to her mother. Everything was labelled, *'Miss R. Wallace, Villa*

Santa Barbara, Malaga.' Enthralling address for Rosemary . . . forbidding and menacing for Miss Bryant.

If only the child were going to any part of England! . . . and not across the water on to the Continent, which held, for Ida, nameless terrors.

Rosemary stood there a moment longer, discussing the journey. It was going to be such fun. She would get to Paris this afternoon and take the express to Madrid, which meant travelling all night. Then on from Madrid to Malaga, which the Señora had told her was a wonderful journey between the famous mountain ranges which separate old from new Castille.

'And the moment I get to Malaga, I'll wire you that I'm safe,' Rosemary concluded.

'Well, mind you take care of yourself,' said Ida dolefully.

Then the guard blew his whistle, and Rosemary jumped into her carriage. There was one more embrace, more promises, good wishes, good-byes. Then

18

the train steamed slowly out of the station. Rosemary waved to her friend as long as she could see her. Gradually the homely figure faded from view. They came out of the dark station into the pale spring sunlight. Rosemary sat down in the corner, and with a throb of the heart thought of that much fiercer sun which would soon shine upon her in another land.

With glistening eyes she looked at the labels on her luggage.

'Villa Santa Barbara!' she murmured. 'Oh, I wonder what life holds for me? I wonder what I shall find waiting for me in Spain?'

After all her eager anticipation and hope she might be disappointed. She might find the Lamandas a stodgy, sticky family, and Mercedes an uncongenial companion. She might even dislike this Spain for which she had so ardently longed.

Rosemary sighed a little, took a Spanish grammar from her suitcase, and settled down in her corner to study it as the train gathered speed and rushed through the April sunlight toward the coast.

Whatever happened it must be better than the monotonous life that she had led at home for the last few years. She felt that a vivid thread of colour was to be woven into the grey fabric of her existence.

Softly she began to repeat to herself a Spanish verb.

★   ★   ★

To Rosemary, who had never travelled before, the journey was interesting from the very beginning. The crossing from Dover to Calais was not too smooth, but she found herself to be a good sailor and sat out on deck with a rug round her, enjoying the fresh strong breeze that whipped the colour into her cheeks and the sight of the blue, dancing Channel waters.

At Calais they passed through the custom-house into the train, and now she felt that the most enthralling part of the adventure was about to begin. She had left England behind her. This was France, and this was the Paris express. What a wealth of romance lay in that word *Paris*, and it was so much more exciting to be able to do this journey in the height of comfort. The letter she had received from Señora Lamanda had told her to travel first class, and that all her expenses would be paid. Rosemary felt almost that she had left her real self behind her in London — in the dreary, dingy office of Messrs. Tring & Sons. This was a new personality, this Rosemary with her chic clothes, her first-class tickets, her luggage, all labelled for Malaga. And then came the Big Moment when, at Paris, she changed into the express for Hendaya, which was the border between France and Spain. Late that night she would change over into yet another train, which would convey her to Madrid. It might have seemed an exhausting journey to a great many people, but

Rosemary, young and buoyant, felt tireless and eager to look at the scenery and enjoy every moment of her travel.

On the French train she was given a carriage to herself, but at the last moment, just before they left the Quai D'Orsay, a porter bustled in with three big leather suitcases plastered with coloured labels, showing that the owner had travelled extensively. An overcoat and some magazines were flung into a corner seat opposite Rosemary. A tall man took that seat, tipped the porter, and almost immediately afterwards the train moved out of the station.

She was a little sorry that she was not, after all, to have the carriage to herself, because it was so nice to put one's feet up and relax. She glanced over the rim of her magazine, and was at once struck by the amazing good looks of her travelling companion. He was quite young, and almost too handsome, Rosemary decided. Rather like one of the film heroes whom poor old Ida found so engaging. But

Rosemary had never been a film 'fan'. On the other hand she had to admire sheer physical beauty, and here it was.

The young man, who had taken off his hat and settled himself down with a newspaper, was tall and well-proportioned. His well-shaped head, with jet-black hair waving thickly back from a fine forehead, might have belonged to some young sculptured god of ancient Greece. Of course he was not English, Rosemary decided. That warm brown skin and long dark eyes with the magnificent lashes could only belong to a foreigner. To a Spaniard, no doubt. One of the 'barbarians' whom Ida disliked so fervently.

At the same time, Rosemary was a little puzzled by the very British grey flannels and college tie which the young man was wearing.

'I wonder who he is,' she thought, and amused herself by trying to make out what was written on his luggage labels. But she could see nothing beyond the word *Malaga*. That was intriguing. He was bound for the same destination as herself!

Rosemary returned to her magazine.

Immediately the young man raised his head from the depths of his paper and cast a critical glance at the girl. And the same question entered his mind. He wondered who she was. But being a man, less inquisitive than a woman, he did not seek for information from her luggage. He merely congratulated himself that the next eight hours were to be spent in the company of a pretty woman. English, of course. The quiet, tasteful tweeds, the sensible brown walking shoes on the small, shapely foot, and the extreme fairness of her skin and hair labelled her English at once. She had taken off her hat, and he thought that blonde graceful head, resting against the square of white linen on the cushioned back of the carriage, altogether charming.

With the eye of a connoisseur he appreciated the graceful lines of her figure, the delicate contour of throat and nose and chin, and the hint of passion in that small red mouth. 'Quite lovely,' he thought, 'and possibly very well off. But why alone? Taking a holiday in Spain, perhaps.' He resolved to find out a little more about her, but for the moment returned discreetly to his newspaper.

The opportunity presented itself when an attendant thrust his head into the carriage and asked if they would take the first or second dinner on the train.

The young man answered in perfect French, Rosemary, a little nervous, stammered and looked helpless. Immediately the young man spoke to her in English as good as his French.

'Can I be of assistance?'

'Oh . . . thank you.' Rosemary blushed and smiled. 'I'm afraid I'm a perfect fool about French.'

'You would like the second dinner?'

'I . . . I suppose so.'

'It passes the time and one must eat.'

He smiled. 'Perhaps you would do me the honour of dining with me?'

Rosemary was a little disconcerted, but told herself that it would be stupid of her to reject the courteous invitation. But she could just imagine Miss Bryant's expression of horror. Already she would imagine her 'lamb' in the wolf's clutches.

As the attendant closed the door, the young man looked at Rosemary with a smile, and said:

'These long journeys can be so boring.'

'Oh, I'm finding it most exciting,' she said.

He raised his brows. He saw now that she was young and very inexperienced. He was more than ever intrigued.

'You haven't done much travelling?'

'None — this is my first trip abroad.'

'How wonderful to be you! I've done this particular journey so often that I feel I know every inch of the route.'

'Do you know Spain well, then?'

'Very well. I am Spanish.'

'I see. But you speak English perfectly.'

'I was at an English public school.'

'I understand.'

Rosemary felt a little relieved. Even Ida could not call this young Spaniard a barbarian, having had such a British education!

'We get to Hendaya just before midnight,' he said. 'I suppose you've got a *wagon-lit* from there?'

'Yes.'

'You're going to stay in Madrid?'

'No. I'm going down to Malaga.'

'Ah, yes; so am I.'

'I am going to a Spanish family — to be companion to a young girl who wishes to learn English.'

'Ah, yes,' he said.

He lowered his gaze. He was a little bored. Disappointing to find this lovely girl only a paid companion. On the other hand she was very young and fresh and charming. He had had rather a lot of the other type of woman lately. Rather too many cocktail parties and dances — passing rapidly from one brief, amusing *affaire de cœur* to another. So many of these girls who sat beside a man on a high stool at a cocktail bar and drank highballs were the same . . experienced, blasé, offering a man lips fresh from another's kisses. He wondered how many had kissed the small beautiful mouth of this girl opposite him? Not many. Perhaps none!

He offered her a cigarette-case. 'Will you have one?'

'Thank you, I don't smoke.'

'How unusual. Do you mind if I do?'

'Not at all.'

He lit the cigarette, and Rosemary was at once fascinated by his hands. They were brown, narrow, with long sensitive fingers. Restless fingers. His whole personality was restless. And he had a trick of running his hand over the back of his head continually. A nervous gesture. Too many late nights; too many drinks; too many cigarettes . . . too many ardours. That was the whole secret of his 'nerves'.

'You'll be glad to get to the sunshine, won't you?' he asked her.

'I'm longing for it.'

'It's glorious in Malaga at this time of the year.'

Then he noted the book on her knee, and smiled. 'Studying my language?'

'Yes.'

He asked her a question in Spanish. She answered shyly, but with some pride, and suddenly he found her delicious.

'That was very good. You have quite a good accent. But you'll learn more after a few weeks in Spain than you would ever do at classes in London.'

'I am thrilled with it,' she said. 'I've always been thrilled by anything Spanish.'

His lips curved in a smile, and he showed white, splendid teeth.

'Does that include a Spaniard . . . like myself?'

'Absurd,' she murmured.

'Well I hope you'll continue to be interested in Spanish things,' he said. 'I think that you'll love my country. It's a queer, savage, beautiful place.'

She began to question him about all the things which fascinated her. And he was quite surprised at her knowledge. She could talk of the painters, the poets, the musicians of Spain. He was amused by her enthusiasm and willing to instruct her. By eight o'clock they were good friends and Rosemary had forgotten to be shy of him, and was finding him a most engaging and amusing companion.

As they walked along the corridor to the dining-car . . . the train swaying and creaking . . . Rosemary stumbled a little, and his hand shot out to steady her. She noted the onyx signet ring on the little finger of his brown hand, and wondered who he was.

'We don't know each other's names yet,' she said.

'Don't let's be too formal,' he said. 'My name's Paul.'

She hesitated a moment. Wasn't this becoming just a little too intimate? But why not? Life was offering adventure indeed, and this young Spaniard was the most attractive man she had ever met. He would think her old-fashioned and dull if she insisted upon the conventions. So she took her cue from him, and answered:

'Mine's Rosemary.'

'For remembrance,' he laughed. 'But how very English . . . and straight from a cottage garden. Rose-Marie . . . charming . . . '

Rose-Marie! He said that with just the merest hint of a foreign inflexion . . . the rolling of the first 'R'. It sounded more attractive from his lips than it had ever sounded to her from anybody else's. And Rose-Marie he called her, always, after that.

The dinner was delightful. Paul took charge of her completely — ordered just what he knew she would want to eat, and insisted upon her sharing a bottle of white wine with him.

Rosemary's mind slipped back to the thought of suppers shared with Ida

— eggs and Camp coffee with condensed milk — in her flat . . . a *5s. 6d.* dinner, with ginger-ale for a treat, in a Soho restaurant. Nothing very romantic had ever happened with Ida. That all seemed like another life now. This was Romance with a capital 'R'. This dinner, in the swaying train as it rushed through the night across France toward the Spanish border, with a dark-eyed, handsome young man called Paul, who raised his glass and toasted her:

'To Rose-Marie.'

It was like a very pleasant dream, and Rosemary enjoyed it to the full.

Back in their carriage, he insisted upon settling her with a cushion at her back and unstrapping his own rug to place over her feet.

'It's chilly travelling, even in the spring,' he said.

She lay back, feeling content and happy.

'What about you?'

'I don't want to lie down just yet.'

He sat back in his corner and

smoked, having first fitted the cigarette into a long onyx holder. Everything he had was expensive, Rosemary noticed. And he behaved as though he were a young man of wealth, used to flinging money about. Who was he? She wished that she knew his other name. He appeared not to wish for more detailed introductions between them. They were to be just Paul and Rose-Marie.

'Let's talk Spanish,' he suggested after a while.

'Oh, but I speak it so badly.'

'No, you don't. And anyhow I'll coach you.'

His long brown eyes, with their rather sleepy, indolent lids, rested on her intently. He was thinking how very desirable she looked, stretched there on the opposite seat, with the dim light in the compartment bringing out the gold in her hair. She had taken off her coat. He could see the beautiful moulding of her throat, the slight curve of her breasts under the organdie blouse. Her skin was marvellously white. He felt a growing desire to stretch out a hand and see how brown his fingers would look against the whiteness of that skin.

'Translate this for me,' he murmured. ''*Te quiero*.''

Her cheeks burned with colour, and her gaze dropped before his. She knew perfectly well what it meant. '*I love thee*.' He was growing bold. Yet, try as she would, she could not still the sudden leaping of her blood and the beating of her heart. He was altogether too fascinating, this young Spaniard. And especially when he spoke in his own language in that liquid, caressing voice.

'Well?' he said teasingly. 'Don't you know what it means?'

'Of course I do.'

'Then tell me.'

'Don't be so ridiculous.'

He laughed, and stubbed his cigarette-end on the window-sill.

'Typically English . . . so cold . . . cold as the snow-peaks of Granada.'

'Not at all.'

'Oh!' His long lashes flickered, and his eyes, dark and brilliant, continued to tease her 'Not at all? Then timid . . . just too timid to say those three such lovely words, 'I love thee.''

'I don't think they come into the usual Spanish lesson,' Rosemary said a little reproachfully.

'Maybe not. But they're the only words that count in *my* grammar.'

'You are absurd.'

'You know,' he continued, 'I love England. I've loved my education over there. But I do think it's a chilly country.'

'Reserved, if you like.'

'Are you very reserved, Rose-Marie?'

'Why — why, yes; I think so.'

'Not sure?'

'Yes, of course I am.'

'So am I!' He followed that with a low laugh.

She could see perfectly well that he was mocking her, and the colour kept on stinging her cheeks. The colour enchanted him. Very few of the women to whom he had made love recently knew how to blush.

He adored the fairness of her hair and her skin. She was really ravishing.

'I must say one never knows what life is going to hold for one,' he said. 'And when I jumped on to this train in Paris I had no idea the journey was going to be so . . . shall we say intriguing? It's the first time for years that I haven't been bored between Paris and Madrid.'

She did not answer. It was so difficult to answer such direct flattery, but her pulse quickened. She just could not help responding. Of course she must be either mad or bad to lie here and allow a complete stranger to talk to her in this manner, but she found it quite impossible to stop him. There was something so boyishly engaging about this brown-faced, dark-eyed Paul.

'Don't you think it's been rather wonderful?' he asked her.

'What?'

'Our meeting like this.'

'I . . . yes . . . it's been lovely.'

'You're lovely,' he said under his breath.

'I . . . I think I'm going to try and sleep,' she said confusedly.

And deliberately she shut her eyes.

Paul stared at her. She looked lovelier than ever like that . . . with long silky lashes curling on her cheeks. He was tempted to lean forward and touch her lips with his. But something held him back. A queer tenderness and regard that her innocence roused in him. After a while those lashes lifted, and the hazel-gold eyes looked up into his again. Rosemary stirred restlessly. It was impossible to sleep. She could almost feel his gaze burning through her closed lids.

'Can't sleep?' he asked.

'No,' she said almost crossly.

'I'm not tired, either. Let's go on talking.'

'What about?'

'You . . . and me . . . and how wonderful it is that we have met like this. Now if it had been at a social tea-party, which God forbid, we'd have just smiled, bowed, said a few words, and walked away. But here we are together, alone, with the night in front of us. And it's so much more intriguing that we don't know anything about each other . . . don't you think so, Rose-Marie . . . ?'

'I think it's all quite . . . quite thrilling,' she said breathlessly.

'Your name suits you. You're so like a flower.'

'I'm not,' she said.

But she felt a queer hot sensation in her throat. This Paul was a sorcerer. He was casting a spell on her with the caress of his eyes and the words which he spoke. She had never known any man to draw her out of herself so completely in so short a while. But, then, how different were the men she had known from Paul! She had to smile at the memory of the dull weedy youths in the office of Tring & Sons . . . the distant, dry personality of her employer . . . in fact the difficult and boring young men whom she met anywhere in London. It wouldn't be easy for one to feel a single thrill for such as these. And Rosemary had begun to believe that real romance, exotic and glowing, such as one saw in cinemas or read in books, was a myth. Yet here it was in reality, close to her, tempting her. And she was just falling, weakly, and she knew it.

'Once we get to Spain we may never meet again,' Paul was saying. 'I wonder what life holds for us, Rose-Marie.'

'I asked myself that when I started this journey.'

'What would you like it to hold?'

'I don't know.'

'Do you know nothing about yourself, you queer, cold little thing?'

'Quite a lot.'

'Have you ever been in love?'

Again she stirred restlessly under his ardent glances.

'N-no; I don't think I have.'

'I don't think you have, either. There's something very like a child about you.'

'But I'm twenty-two.'

'I'm two years older than that, and look it. You might be eighteen. It amazes me that with such a face, such a figure as yours, some man has not snapped you up long ago.'

'I've had one proposal,' she admitted.

'A thrilling one?'

She laughed outright. Thrilling! She thought of the dull and staid young man, a clerk in Messrs. Tring & Sons, who had taken her to Richmond in his sidecar one summer's evening and asked her to wait for him. To wait for what? The life of a household drudge in some suburb, with never enough money to enjoy life on, and children whom one couldn't afford to educate. No, she hadn't accepted that proposal, and hadn't even been moved to give the young man the embrace he had asked for. She said:

'I didn't care about him. I've never cared about anybody.'

'But you could . . . you could care

very much . . . if you fell in love.'

Her lashes fluttered. 'I think so, yes.'

'I am sure of it.'

'What about you?' she asked him suddenly. 'Let's talk about you for a change.'

★ ★ ★

The train rushed on, screaming shrilly at intervals through the night, racing through Orleans, on to Bordeaux, toward Biarritz.

In the warm, quiet first-class compartment shared by Paul and Rosemary, the queer intimate conversation went on. The atmosphere was strangely intense, and these two young people, who had only met a few hours ago, looked into each other's eyes as though they were both seeking to solve the riddle of Life itself.

Paul was talking about himself. There was a frown on his handsome face. A slight bitterness in his eyes. A cynical twist to his handsome mouth.

'If I ever really fell in love, Rose-Marie, it would be so madly that I would lose all sense of proportion. I admit it. There are times when my Spanish blood burns in me and all my British upbringing counts for nothing. I don't think I have ever loved like that . . . yet.'

'Perhaps you will when you meet the woman you mean to marry.'

'Marry!' He gave an altogether cynical laugh. 'My dear child, marriage won't necessarily mean real love for me! But I don't want even to discuss that.'

She wondered then what had happened to make him so hard, so bitter. Much too bitter for a boy of twenty-four.

He said:

'I don't want to discuss myself any more at all. I want to go on talking about you.'

'No . . . I am so ordinary . . . '

'So extraordinary. More like a fragrant flower than anything I've ever seen or met.'

'You say such lovely things.'

'Only to such a lovely person as yourself.'

'Oh, but I'm not!'

His brown eyes were suddenly hungry as they rested on her fair, shining head. Her cheeks, even her throat now, were carnation pink.

And suddenly he leaned forward. Rosemary felt warm strong fingers grip her wrists. He whispered: 'Ah, Rose-Marie . . . '

She tried to draw her hands away.

'Don't,' he said. 'Don't be cold with me. And don't be afraid. I won't hurt you.'

'I'm not afraid . . . '

She said the words bravely, but she was not at all sure that she meant them. She was really more frightened than she had ever been in her life . . . of herself . . . of the queer, dominating influence of this man, and of the wild way in which her heart was pounding. She looked up into his eyes, and felt herself lost, drowning, slipping into a world which was altogether unreal.

'Rose-Marie,' he said, and knelt beside her now. 'It will be an hour or two more before we get to Hendaya, and then twelve long ones before we come to Madrid. Why shouldn't they be unforgettable, marvellous hours for us both?'

'Oh, what do you mean?'

His arms were round her now. He was drawing her close to him. She could feel his strong, sensitive fingers burning through her thin organdie blouse.

'No, please . . . '

'Let me kiss you, Rose-Marie.'

'No!' she cried again, and tried to be that sane, normal, practical Rosemary who had lived a very dull and ordinary life in London and had known neither love nor lover. She tried and failed, altogether bewitched by the hour, and conscious of a wild hunger to take what the gods . . . what this god was offering her.

She could almost hear Ida Bryant

cautioning her in horror ... hear herself talking to Ida about life, scornful of girls who slipped into crazy love-affairs with men they scarcely knew ...

She was scornful of herself, but could not stem the tide that was engulfing her now. However much she was to regret it in the future, and whatever life was to hold, she could not fight against Paul nor the intoxication of his love-making, which was beautiful and fervent, and more wonderful than anything about which she had ever dreamed.

He was smoothing the fair tumbled hair away from her forehead.

'I am bewitched, and so are you. Don't you feel the spell, Rose-Marie? Won't you ... '

'Oh, I ... I do,' she panted. 'But please, Paul, let me go.'

'You don't really want me to ... '

The brown, boyish, ardent face was close to hers now. 'Rose-Marie, won't you kiss me? Won't you thaw a little ... love me a little, just for to-night?'

She was as white now as she had

been rosy. Her body trembled in his embrace. Of course she was mad, and so was he. Bewitched he called it, and perhaps he was right. But in a few short hours she had fallen in love for the first time in her life. Her golden eyes were bright and terrified, but her lips were half open, like a red chalice lifted for the sacrifice.

'Rose-Marie, *te quiero* . . . I love thee,' he whispered.

Then his arms tightened about her with a fierce little gesture of passion. His lips took what her red mouth offered. She gave a little choking cry and surrendered to the long madness of that kiss.

Something wakened in her then that could never sleep again. And it was not merely the intoxication of a moment, but the passion of a lifetime. There was to be no other man on earth for her, except this man, Paul. She was obliterated by his love and his passion.

The train rushed on . . . again and again he kissed her, and his ardour was a flame which lit a responsive one in her until they were lost and burning in each other's arms.

His slim brown hands threaded through the gold of her hair, and her arms were curved about his neck. Again and again he whispered:

'I love you, Rose-Marie . . . ' And in Spanish he repeated the words and made her answer him:

'*Te quiero, mucho* . . . much.'

She meant it. She gave him her heart with both small feverish hands that fevered hour. She was no longer Rosemary Wallace . . . she was a new Rosemary, to whom life meant only Paul.

And then suddenly he seemed to change, at least so she thought. He ceased to kiss her with those slow, devouring kisses which burnt her body and brain. He let her go and sat back in his seat, and for a moment covered his face with his hands. She, breathless, starry-eyed, watched him, and whispered:

47

'Paul. What is it, darling Paul?'

He did not answer her. He smoothed back his dark ruffled hair with that restless, characteristic gesture, and lit a cigarette, putting it first in the long holder which was now familiar to her.

Some of the madness left Rosemary. Rapture gave place to sudden doubt. The fine edge of her ecstasy was blunted.

Perhaps he did not love her. He had said: 'Love me a little, just for to-night.' Perhaps he had meant that. Just for to-night and no longer.

The idea of that shattered her completely. Perhaps he had played this game before, this handsome and intriguing young Spaniard. To her it wasn't quite such an idle game. She had never been made love to by any man before, and had never even imagined herself capable of loving anybody so wildly.

She was beginning to learn her lesson . . . to run the gamut of all the emotions rolled into one. And suddenly she felt sick of the pain of loving . . . and she lay very still, with closed eyes, and thought:

'I wish I could die now . . . die before this ends . . . '

When he spoke to her again it was almost formally.

'You should really try and sleep a little. You will be so tired.'

She took her cue from him, too proud to make any appeal.

'Yes, I'll try and sleep.'

But of course that was out of the question. She shut her eyes, but sleep was far from her, and her brain was dizzy with feverish thought. She only knew that she wanted more than anything in the world to feel the touch of his hands upon her and the madness of his lips on hers again.

They travelled in dead silence for the rest of the journey to Hendaya. There, Paul was courteous and attentive; piloted her through the customs, tipped the porters, found her compartment in the *wagon-lit*.

It was number thirteen. For the first time that struck her as being unlucky. She was cold and pale, and dreadfully unhappy, when finally she sat on the edge of the bed in the tiny compartment, and looked at Paul, who stood in the doorway, looking down at her.

'My number is fifteen . . . just two away from yours,' he said.

'I . . . hope you sleep well,' she said in a choked voice.

'One never does in these trains . . . it's very noisy and uncomfortable, I think,' he said. 'We will meet in the morning. Then you must let me drive you across Madrid and help you into the train for Malaga. There are so many changes, and really it is rather confusing for a stranger.'

A stranger! Yes, she felt like one to him, now. It was horrible, and yet an hour ago, lying in his arms in that other train, she had felt nearer to him than she had been to anybody on earth.

She took off her beret. Mutely her

hazel eyes questioned him. And suddenly tears glistened on her lashes.

That seemed to move him to sudden action. With a bewildering change of front he became the Paul who had been her passionate lover. He came into the small room, closed the door, and for an instant took her in his arms.

'Sweet, lovely little thing . . . Rose-Marie . . . sweet Rose-Marie!'

He covered her face and throat and hair with kisses.

Relief surged through her, and she surrendered madly to his caresses.

'You're adorable,' he said. 'And I adore you.'

'I love you, Paul . . . '

'I shall never forget you,' he said. 'Never; never.'

And then as suddenly his mood changed again, and he released her and stood up and bade her an almost formal good night.

The door closed upon him. She almost sprang to her feet and followed him. Then she told herself not to be a little fool. She was conscious suddenly of overpowering fatigue. Her eyelids burned. She was trembling like one in a fever. It was, indeed, as though she had passed through a terrific storm. An emotional storm. And she was rent in twain by it. She could never be the same Rosemary again.

If only she could understand this queer, passionate Spaniard. But he was so difficult to understand. She could only take it for granted that he did not really love her ... that he was just temporarily amused by her. He had not even asked her surname, nor to whom she was going, neither had he suggested that they would ever meet again.

She crept into bed and turned off the light. The train creaked and jolted. The narrow bed seemed hard. All the thrill of the journey had gone ... all the excitement. She felt dreadfully unhappy. Of course she had been crazy to allow Paul to make love to her. She began to realise that although he was a born lover, the most charming, the most marvellous that a woman could want, there was something hard and cruel behind that delightful mask. Yes, now she came to think of it, that well-shaped mouth of his was cruel. She would come up against a stone wall if she so much as suggested that he should not say good-bye, and that they should meet again.

Of course she wouldn't say anything. She must have more pride than that. But she would have to school herself for to-morrow. It would not be easy to bid a formal farewell to him, and to realise that she would never see him again.

She slept badly. And she was up and dressed long before the train steamed into Madrid. She sat on the edge of the narrow bed in the *wagon-lit*, staring out of the big window at the outskirts of the Spanish capital, caught her first glimpse of whitewashed houses, white walls gay with bougainvillaea, palm trees, *Spain*! Yes, here at last was the Spain for which she had longed, and about which she had dreamed. And it was all spoiled.

The landscape was blotted by a mist of tears.

Two compartments away was Paul . . . and she was in love, and he had just played a game. What a little fool she had been!

'Spoiled!' she whispered to herself. 'All spoiled; oh, how cruel!'

Just as the train was coming to a standstill, Paul made his appearance. His brown handsome face looked tired and older in the bright morning sunlight, and he was unsmiling, even stern. He looked at Rosemary only for a fleeting moment, then looked away again.

'We're here,' he said. 'Can I see you safely into the Malaga train? I shall not be going on it myself, as I have business in Madrid and I am catching a later one.'

Rosemary's face was very white. For one mad moment she wanted to fling herself into his arms and beg him not to leave her like this; remind him of all the passionate words he had poured into her ear only yesterday. But she said nothing at all like that. She spoke with an indifference borrowed from him:

'Thanks, it's kind of you, but I'm sure I can manage myself. Good-bye, Señor . . . ?' She paused on an upward inflexion of the voice, demanding, a trifle sarcastically, his name.

For an instant Paul's dark eyes burned down into hers, then he gave a bitter little smile and bowed.

'Paul let it remain . . . Pablo in Spain. And you will remain in my memory as just — Rose-Marie.'

He held out a hand, but with a feeling of incredible pain she turned from him. This was too much. He was just playing an old game. She could not even say the word 'good-bye.' She leaned out of the window and hailed a porter.

He looked after her. A worried, remorseful look contracted his fine features. Then he shrugged his shoulders in a hopeless way and lit the inevitable cigarette.

Late that same afternoon, Rosemary reached Malaga, the gay, sunny watering-place in the south . . . that golden Andalusia where the peasants work a little, play a little, always with a song on their lips and that word *mañana* . . . which means to-morrow. It was always to-morrow, and never to-day.

Rosemary tried hard to be interested in the town once she was in the big luxurious car which the Lamandas had sent for her. But she was tired and profoundly depressed. For all her endeavours she found it impossible to blot out the memory of Paul and that brief hour of mad passion in his arms.

If only it had never happened! If only she had never met him. In his ardent, supremely selfish fashion, he had taken her to the very gates of heaven with him, only to leave her high and dry . . . to descend into that small hell which only women who love in vain can suffer.

She kept telling herself that she was a fool even to remember him. But Rosemary, intense of nature, was not one to give her heart lightly, and, having given it to this man whose name she did not even know, she was lost. She could not enjoy any of the things which should have been so wonderful to-day.

She did, indeed, cheer up a little when she saw the Lamandas' home. Driving through the big wrought-iron gateway was a revelation. The sun beat down from the cloudless blue sky, still hot and radiant in spite of the fact that it was late afternoon. It seemed impossible to believe that forty-eight hours ago she had been in London, still cold, with the weak and timid sunshine of an English April. Here were great green palms and the feathery bluish jade of eucalyptus, the queer gnarled branches of a cork-tree, the brilliant colours of exotic flowers, and finally a low-built white house, with a wide veranda covered by trailing passion flowers and two great oleanders, in full bloom, as sentinels beside the steps.

The Villa Santa Barbara.

Rosemary felt a brief thrill as she stepped out of the car and felt the warmth of the sun drench her and caught a glimpse of white terraces beyond the garden, then blue sea, purple blue; and beyond, purple mountains and the snow-covered peaks of the Sierra Nevada.

'This is really lovely!' she thought.

But almost immediately came the thought: 'If only *he* were here . . . oh, Paul, Paul!'

Two women appeared in the doorway. Stiff black figures . . . Rosemary was to grow used to the perpetual black worn by the women in Spain. They were always in mourning for some relation or other.

The women came forward and introduced themselves as the Señora Lamanda and an old aunt, an unsmiling nun-like figure, who wore a cross on her bosom and had a proud, almost menacing face. Rosemary immediately took a dislike to her, but the Señora Lamanda herself was pleasant and courteous, and greeted her with some show of warmth.

Nevertheless Rosemary found both the Spanish ladies a little too formal and awe-inspiring, and she hoped her future companion, Mercedes, was not the same.

Inside the villa did not appeal to the English girl. It was large and cool, all stone floors and tiled walls, and rather like a museum, full of heavy Spanish antiques.

Then Rosemary was conducted upstairs and presented to the daughter of the house, who was waiting for her in a small and rather more comfortable-looking room, which was to be Rosemary's boudoir.

Mercedes, a fair Spaniard, proved to be as ravishingly pretty as her photograph. At eighteen she was much more mature than English girls of that age, plump, yet graceful, with a camellia-like skin. Her hair, glossy and pure golden, was wound in two long plaits about her head. But her eyes were truly Spanish — dark, with black lashes of incredible length. Her worst feature was her mouth, which was a little thick and sensuous, and her expression was discontented, even a little furtive. It was not a face which one would trust.

Rosemary was not bothering about the character of the Spanish girl, however. At the moment she was glad to see somebody nearer her own age, and to realise that Mercedes was not as chilly or terrifying as the older ladies of the house.

Mercedes eyed Rosemary with evident pleasure.

'I am so glad you have come,' she said in her own language. 'I'll come and talk to you while you unpack. What is your Christian name?'

'Rosemary.'

'Rose-Marie,' repeated Mercedes.

A little tremor went through the English girl, and her teeth closed over her lower lip. No, she was not going to allow anybody to pronounce the name *that* way. She said:

'You put the accent on the 'Rose' — *Rosemary*.'

Mercedes took her into the adjoining room, which was to be Rosemary's bedroom. It was all in white, and, although stiff and even austere, the view from the window was marvellous. Rosemary looked out, and admired it all.

'How glorious it is here!'

'I'm sick to death of it,' said the Spanish girl, and began to pour a torrent of words into Rosemary's ear. Rosemary smiled, and said:

'Slower, please, or I can't understand you.'

Mercedes pouted.

'But it is such a relief to have somebody to talk to. I dare not tell anything to my mother and the old Aunt Maria. Poof, she gets on my nerves. She is steeped in her religion, and goes to Mass every day. My mother is under her thumb. My father, who understood me, is dead. I was educated in Madrid, and I have modern ideas, and my mother doesn't understand me.'

'Poor little thing,' said Rosemary, at once all sympathy. 'But I understood from your other aunt in London that you were engaged to be married. You will soon be able to leave here and have a home of your own, won't you?'

Mercedes gave a furtive glance about her, then drew closer to Rosemary.

'I don't want to marry him,' she whispered. 'I dread it . . . dread it!'

'Aren't you in love with him, then?'

'No. He is handsome and rich, and many women in Spain are mad about him. But he has a cruel nature. I have heard much about him. I shall never be happy with him. He doesn't love me.'

'Then why on earth are you marrying him?'

'Our families have arranged it. His father and mine wished for the two families to be united, and since children

62

it has been taken for granted. Oh, but Rose-Marie . . . ' — again she pronounced the name as Paul had pronounced it — 'but I am unhappy.'

'I can quite understand that,' said Rosemary gravely. 'Thank God we don't arrange marriages in England.'

'Without love, it will be terrible,' said the Spanish girl.

Rosemary nodded. Yes, marriage without love would be terrible. She knew that. She, who yesterday had learned the meaning of passion, was well aware that she could never marry without love.

'I will show you a photograph of my fiancé,' said Mercedes.

Rosemary sat on the edge of the bed, and, with a little comb, arranged the fair waves of her hair.

'I must wire poor old Ida,' she thought, 'and let her know that I am safely here.'

Mercedes came running back with a large framed photograph, which she thrust into Rosemary's hand.

'This is Pablo, my future husband. 'Paul' you call it in English.'

Pablo! Rosemary's heart jumped, and the blood surged into her cheeks, then receded, leaving her deathly white. Paul, that name which she had whispered so many times clasped in a lover's passionate embrace. A feeling of horror came over her as she looked at the photograph. That sculptured face and head, so flawlessly handsome, were they not unmistakable? This was Paul — her Paul of the train — *her* Paul.

Mercedes was chattering like a magpie beside her.

'That is he. Don Pablo Iballo . . . the Iballos are fabulously wealthy . . . everybody says it's a marvellous match for me. He has properties in Spain and Barcelona, and a villa here in Malaga. He is handsome, is he not? But look at his lips. Don't you think they are cruel? Do you like his face, Rose-Marie?'

Rosemary could not answer. Her mouth, her throat, felt dry. Her hands were hot and shaking. Didn't she like his face? God, hadn't she kissed every inch of it? Wasn't it engraven on her heart for ever? So *he* was the promised husband of Mercedes Lamanda! It was ironic. But the more she thought about it the more bitter she became. Paul had known perfectly well that he was engaged to be married when he had made love to her in that mad, exacting fashion. He had had no right . . . no right to do it. She would never, never have allowed him to make love to her if he had told her first that he was going to marry this girl.

'He is charming to me . . . he is charming to everyone,' Mercedes continued, 'but he has no heart. It is well known that he has been the lover of many women.'

Rosemary nodded speechlessly. Every nerve was jarred. Oh, yes, she could imagine that Paul had been the lover of many women. He was so experienced.

'I could almost kill him,' Rosemary whispered to herself.

He had told her in the train that he

adored fair hair. Well, Mercedes was fair enough. And they were both small, with delicate ankles and hands. Paul had also said that he adored hazel eyes . . . but the eyes of the girl whom he was going to marry were as black as his own.

He was nothing but a philanderer, a cad.

After Mercedes had departed and left her alone to change her dress, Rosemary lay down on her bed for a moment with her face pressed to the pillow. It was no use giving way to her feelings — a mad desire to leave Spain and rush back to England and forget all these people. It was a horrid shock to know that Paul was the fiancé of Mercedes. And of course she would be bound to meet Paul again here . . . that would be almost unbearable. And how would he like it . . . what would be his feelings when he discovered that she was Mercedes' paid companion?

There was only one thing for her to do and that was to face up to the whole business. No doubt she would get over it in time. But she felt as though something had died within her and she could never be the same Rosemary again.

She sent the wire to Ida: *'Arrived safely. All well.'*

And after she had sent it she thought of those words — 'all well' — which were to comfort her devoted friend, and she felt that her heart would break.

For the next couple of days she was fortunately too busy to have time to brood over things. There was much to do. Mercedes began English lessons at once. She wanted to talk English because her fiancé was educated in England, she told Rosemary. That was the worst of it. Rosemary could not get away from the memory of Paul. Mercedes talked of him all day.

And of course the dreaded moment when Rosemary was to see him again came quickly enough. At the end of forty-eight hours, Señora Lamanda arranged a dance at the Villa Santa Barbara to celebrate the return of her future son-in-law to Spain.

Rosemary tried hard to escape. Wouldn't the family prefer that she kept to her own room? she asked. But Mercedes insisted upon Rosemary being present.

'You will enjoy it,' she said. 'And I want you to meet Pablo and tell me what you think of him.'

Rosemary knew already well enough what she thought of Paul!

She felt cold with nerves, and miserably unhappy, at the dance that night. It was quite a glittering affair — a little stiff and formal, perhaps — attended by most of the well-known Spanish families in the district, and all young girls with their *duennas*.

The big *salon* was lit by dozens of electric candles, and full of exotic flowers. There was an orchestra specially imported from Madrid and a general atmosphere of festivity.

Rosemary wore one of her new evening dresses, and, although it was not as expensive as the lovely white embroidered gown worn by Mercedes, it was attractive and suited her to perfection. Her skin and hair looked marvellously fair contrasted with the dark blue chiffon, which had a frilled skirt and a little blue cape with a bow on the right shoulder. She remembered how gaily she had chosen that frock with old Ida. Little had she dreamed that she would put it on in fear and trembling, shrinking from the very thought of her first party in Spain.

Long before he noticed her, Rosemary saw Paul. He was half a head taller than any other man in the ballroom. He looked extraordinarily handsome in the cream uniform of a Spanish officer which he wore on 'State occasions' — cream with gold and scarlet facings.

How well it suited his magnificent figure! With a sharp sensation of pain, Rosemary watched him smile and bow over the hands of several women in the room. Every smile, every flash of his eyes, was so familiar now. He was charming. Nobody knew better than she how charming. And now she also knew that he was ruthless and cruel.

She tried to avoid recognition, but suddenly he saw her, and paused, amazed. She slipped from the room on to the moonlit terrace facing the sea. In a bewildered way he followed the slim figure in blue.

'Rose-Marie!' he cried. '*You!*'

A shiver ran through her at the sound of her name on his lips. But when she turned to him she held herself very stiffly. She gave a formal little bow.

'Don Pablo!' she said.

'You,' he repeated. 'Why are you here?'

'I am teaching English to your future wife,' she said coldly. But her hands, clasped behind her back, were trembling.

'You mean that it was to the Lamandas you were journeying when we met?'

'Yes.'

'Good God, what a coincidence!' he exclaimed.

'Wasn't it?' said Rosemary with a frozen smile, and turned to go. But he caught her arm and detained her.

'Rose-Marie . . . don't go like that . . . why speak to me in such an unfriendly way?'

'You're mistaken, Don Pablo, if you think I intend to make a fool of myself again . . . '

He frowned.

'Rose-Marie . . . were they so foolish . . . those lovely hours?'

'Don't dare!' she broke in. 'You are enaged to Mercedes.'

He bit his lip.

'Rose-Marie, you don't understand . . . in Spain we do these things . . . we sometimes have to marry . . . as our families wish . . . I promised my father on his deathbed that I would come back to Malaga and marry Mercedes and settle down.'

'An excellent plan,' said Rosemary. 'And meanwhile you want amusement, but *I* don't intend to amuse you any longer.'

71

'Rose-Marie . . . '

'Good night,' she interrupted.

Paul stared at her. His Southern blood ran hotly in his veins in this moment. She was beautiful and desirable. He had not forgotten the sweetness of her lips, or her shy surrender. He was spoiled, and not used to being thwarted. His eyes grew suddenly fierce.

'I won't let you go . . . like that, Rose-Marie . . . '

And he caught her recklessly, and held her for a moment against him. Her fair head just reached the ribboned medals on his white uniform. His dark head bent down to her.

'Kiss me again . . . as you did . . . in the train . . . '

'You cad . . . I hate you,' she panted, and struck him across the mouth.

A ring on her finger cut his lower lip. It began to bleed. He released her, and slowly wiped the blood away with a silk handkerchief. His face was ivory white in the moonlight. White with rage. But his eyes were inscrutable. In this moment Rosemary saw that quality of ruthless cruelty in him of which Mercedes had spoken. She gave a smothered sob, turned and ran from the terrace, leaving him alone.

She was quite certain that Don Pablo would hate her now — would never forgive her for that blow.

She had saved her own pride, yet, once she was alone, pride was in tatters. The tears streamed down her face. The real woman in her had wanted to respond when Paul had taken her in his arms — yes, just as she had responded in the train. She hated him — yet loved him. She was conscious of an ache that could never be appeased, of a bitterness that would spoil things for ever. And it would be impossible for her ever to believe in love, in a man, again.

She ran blindly through the beautiful, moon-drenched gardens to the lowest terrace. She wanted to be alone. She could not go back to the dance. But she only found herself blundering into a

73

pair of lovers — a lovely girl in a white dress, clasped in the arms of a dark-haired boy who was not in evening-dress and obviously not one of the party.

Rosemary paused, embarrassed at having interrupted a passionate embrace. Then, to her surprise and distress, she saw that the girl in white was Mercedes, with her pale, lovely face bathed in tears.

'Oh, Rose-Marie!' she said. 'Now you've found me out! But you mustn't tell my mother . . . you mustn't give me away . . . '

'But of course not, my dear,' said Rosemary.

Mercedes clung to the arm of the young man.

'Rose-Marie, now you know my secret. I dread marrying Pablo, because I love Manuel Cadozza. This is Manuel . . . '

Rosemary looked gravely at the young man, who bowed to her in a rather nervous way. He was a good-looking Spaniard, obviously more gentle, more simple, than Paul. Mercedes confessed, there and then, that she and Manuel adored each other. He was a musician from an hotel in Madrid. They had been meeting secretly for weeks. He had little money. He was only a poor violinist. The Lamandas would never accept him. But Mercedes declared that she would die of a broken heart on the day she was given in marriage to Paul.

'Manuel is so sweet, so tender, so understanding, Rose-Marie!' she cried. 'He is utterly different from Pablo, and he worships me.'

'That is so,' said Manuel Cadozza fervently. 'I would give my life for her . . .'

She was intensely sorry for the young couple. She wished she could help them. But what could she do? And when she thought of Paul . . . Paul who was so devilishly fascinating and so cruel . . . she pitied this Spanish girl who loved her young musician.

'We must think out some scheme, some plan, to help you, Mercedes,' said Rosemary. 'Come with me now, please, my dear, in case you are discovered.'

Mercedes flung herself into her young lover's arms. Rosemary turned away. She heard Manuel say:

'*Alma de mi vida.*'

It cut through Rosemary like a knife. Paul had held her, thus, had called her that — 'Soul of my life' — only a few days ago. She felt hurt, raw with the pain of memories. She did not risk another meeting with Paul that night. She went straight to her room, and nobody missed her or asked that she should reappear.

2

A month passed before Rosemary and Paul met again. He was Mercedes' fiancé, but he seemed to have no great wish to be with her, and saw little of her. The girl was desperately unhappy, and, now that Rosemary was in her confidence, talked of nothing, day and night, but Manuel, Manuel!

Rosemary's heart ached for her. The wedding-day was drawing nearer. The Señora took her daughter to Madrid to buy her trousseau. Mercedes was told that Paul had bought both licence and ring, and was preparing to marry her on the last day of May. It was now only a fortnight off.

Mercedes grew desperate, and Rosemary more and more bitter. Paul had hurt her so badly. Why — why should he be allowed to marry this girl who loved Manuel Cadozza . . .

and ruin her whole life?

The two girls, walking to the village along the white road that fringed the cliff, one hot still afternoon, met a green and silver car bearing the crest of the Iballos. It pulled up beside them. Paul sat at the wheel. A strangely English Paul, to-day, in white flannels and college scarf. He had been playing tennis with friends.

He avoided Rosemary's eye. He gave all his attention to Mercedes; kissed her hand; paid her charming compliments. Only when the car moved off again, he let his inscrutable eyes rest on Rosemary. Her heart gave a queer, fierce throb. How dared he look at her so? A look that almost mocked her . . . challenged her.

'I hate him,' said Mercedes miserably as they walked on. 'Oh, Rose-Marie, why can't I run away with Manuel?'

'I hate him too,' Rosemary thought. But she suffered for the rest of that day and night, at the remembrance of him.

There came at last the wedding-day

of Mercedes and Paul.

In a blaze of sunlight, Don Pablo and his best man drove to the church in Malaga to await the bride. Paul wore his white uniform, and one brown, nervous hand rested on the hilt of his sword. His handsome face was bored. The church would be crammed with elegant people. The marriage was a fashionable one. Young Iballo was carrying out a promise to his father. His mother, now dead, had been half English. It was at her wish that Paul had been educated in England. But the late Don Iballo had asked that his son and heir should finally return to his native land and settle down with the daughter of Lamanda, who had been old Iballo's greatest friend.

So Paul was on his way to church to-day to keep his word. But he could not concentrate on the thought of the brown-eyed Spanish girl. Bitterly, even furiously, with all the passion of his race, he remembered a slim, hazel-eyed English girl who had struck him across the mouth. He hated her for that. He wanted her, too!

In her bedroom, in the Villa Santa Barbara, the prospective bride stood in her shimmering satin robes, her fair head bowed under a crown of pearls and orange flowers, and a veil of thick, Spanish lace. She wept bitterly. She was alone with her paid companion.

Downstairs, the Señora and Aunt Maria were giving final orders. Conte Lamanda, Mercedes' uncle, waited to give his niece away. Rosemary, in a white dress and big hat, was permitted to attend the wedding. She felt that she was going to a funeral. She hated the idea of seeing Paul united to Mercedes — for a dozen conflicting reasons. But at least, after it was over, she could leave Spain and return to England. Gone now were all her former longings for Spain. Her one desire was to get back to London . . . to forget.

Mercedes clung to her.

'Oh, Rose-Marie, Rose-Marie, I'm so miserable . . . if only it were to Manuel

I was going to be married. Rose-Marie, they'll call for me in a moment. I can't marry Pablo — I *can't*!'

Rosemary stood silent, pale, preoccupied. For a few moments she did not speak, but pressed Mercedes' hand in sympathetic silence. Wild schemes were chasing through her brain. She was seized, suddenly, at the eleventh hour before this marriage, with a wild spirit of adventure.

'Rose-Marie, I can't go through with it,' sobbed Mercedes. 'Last night, when I said good-bye to Manuel, he said he would throw himself into the sea to-night, when he pictured me in Pablo's arms.'

Rosemary was smitten with that vision, also, and shivered uncontrollably. Why — why should that handsome devil of a man make Mercedes for ever miserable and be responsible for a warm-hearted boy's suicide?

'Listen, Mercedes,' she said rapidly, in Spanish, 'I have a plan.'

Mercedes' eyes, glittering with tears,

stared at Rosemary.

'*Madre de Dios*, how can you save me now?'

'I can if you are brave enough to risk it . . . for Manuel.'

'I'd risk anything on earth for him. I can't think why I didn't run away with him, money or no money, last night.'

'Then change places with me.'

'With you — but *how, how*, Rose-Marie?'

'We are the same height, and we both have fair hair. With that thick lace veil over my face nobody would know I was not you.'

Mercedes caught her breath.

'*Santa Maria* . . . what are you suggesting, Rose-Marie?'

'Just that we change clothes. I will go to church and marry Don Pablo to-day in your place. You, in my things, can slip away out of the back door — and go to your Manuel. The church is only a few miles away. I will drive there in your place. I need not speak. I can pretend to be crying . . . '

Mercedes trembled violently.

'But Rose-Marie, what a *marvellous* plan! Manuel will be in his hotel . . . if I go to him he will almost die of ecstasy.'

'Then go to him, *querida*, and take your happiness. Don't marry a man you hate,' said Rosemary.

'But what about you?'

'The marriage will not be legal. It will be annulled, of course, immediately it is discovered. And it will be a fine thing to see Don Pablo's discomfiture when he lifts my veil and sees who I am.'

Mercedes tore off her orange wreath, rushed to her bedroom door and locked it. Her cheeks were red; her eyes shining.

'Oh, Rose-Marie, Rose-Marie, I'll let you do this mad thing — I must — I must go to Manuel. I realise now that I would rather have him and lose everything else.'

'How lucky you are to be so much in love,' said Rosemary.

'One day you will meet some man to make you happy, darling Rose-Marie,' said the Spanish girl.

Rosemary did not answer. But as she stepped out of her white dress and put on Mercedes' bridal robe of heavy satin, and Mercedes affixed the pearl-embroidered train to her shoulders, her heart was full of bitterness. A man to make her happy! No, that would never be. There was only the man who had made her unhappy. Don Pablo Iballo. It would be a fine revenge for her. He would seethe with anger, with chagrin, when he discovered the trick — when he realised he had married the little English companion who had *amused* him in the train. Of course, the ceremony would not be legal. He could get rid of her at once. But she wouldn't care. She'd just go back to England . . . and try to forget . . . Paul.

It was a daring, dangerous thing to do. But Rosemary did it, and carried out her rôle skilfully, buoyed by the feeling that she had, at least, brought happiness to poor little Mercedes. At the very moment when Manuel Cadozza held his adored Mercedes in a feverish embrace, Rosemary Wallace walked up the church aisle on Conte Lamanda's arm — to all appearances, Mercedes, his niece.

Don Pablo gave one bored glance at the procession as it drew near him. He was momentarily struck by the grace and beauty of the young figure in the satin and pearl dress, but he was barely thrilled. He could not see her face through the thick veil. He only caught a gleam of golden hair when the glittering candle-lights from the altar fell upon her.

Rosemary stood beside Paul on the chancel step.

She shook from head to foot. She had felt the strangest sensation when she walked down the church towards Paul's splendid figure in the white uniform, with decorations blazing on his breast. When the great organ trembled into muffled music, the solemnity of the whole atmosphere struck her, overawed her. She was filled with grief. She had loved this man so passionately. In the train, half the night long she had sat beside him; his arm about her and her head against his heart, and had felt that heart beat madly for her. His lips had crushed hers in passion, in ecstasy. For one blinding moment she imagined herself in reality his bride.

But in a short while the farce would end and he would hate her even more than he already hated her. He would order her out of his sight.

Paul felt the bridal figure beside him shiver, and thought:

'Poor little Mercedes. She is no happier than I am. I must try to be good to her, poor child . . . '

And he whispered:

'Give me your hand, *querida mia* . . . '

Rosemary gave him her hand. Like slender bands of steel his brown fingers grasped her white one. A queer look shot into his handsome, bored eyes. But she did not see it.

The rest of the ceremony was a dream — his clear responses — her whispered ones. In the guise of Mercedes Lamanda she was united by three priests to Pablo Juan Fernando Iballo.

In the vestry she signed Mercedes' name. Paul added his signature firmly, then suddenly took her in his arms.

'Our bridal kiss, *alma de mi vida*,' he said.

Alma de mi vida! That name again. In a panic she clung to her veil. He laughed, and kissed her through it. His lips, burning like fire through the mist of lace, sent the blood coursing wildly through her veins.

'It's time he knew who I was,' she thought. 'He is shameless. He would make love even to Mercedes, who bores him.'

She found herself in the vivid sunlight, clinging to the bridegroom's arm. She saw, as in a daze, a sea of brown faces, heard tumultuous cheering:

'*Viva!* . . . Iballo . . . Lamanda. *Viva! Ollé!*'

She remembered that Mercedes had told her she would not have to face the family at once. She would carry out old traditions. When an Iballo married, he took his bride straight from the church to his home. Rosemary, therefore, found herself being lifted by Paul into his green and silver car. The door slammed. The car moved forward, driven by a chauffeur in the Iballo livery. They were bound for Paul's magnificent villa, which had been built two hundred years ago in a wild, remote part of the mountains behind Malaga.

Paul sat back in the car. Rosemary looked at him, her heart pounding, her face as white now as her veil. She tried to speak — to tell him who she was and what she had done, and words failed her. She was suddenly, overwhelmingly afraid of this man.

He lifted her hand, on which a moment ago he had slipped a diamond circlet, and raised it to his lips. She trembled and shrank back.

'You are afraid of me, *querida*,' he murmured, in his most caressing voice. 'Do not be afraid . . . '

Rosemary felt tongue-tied. He had said that to her in the train — in just such a voice. Perhaps he imagined himself in love with his wife — for the amusement of a moment. She was fiercely glad she was going to disappoint him. Yet still no words came from her. She sat there with her hand locked in his, trembling face hidden by the lace.

They came to a wonderful white villa, which was like a little palace in its splendid, terraced garden. The grounds were beautiful, with tall palm-trees pointing to the sky. There were masses of roses and carnations here, pink and scarlet and gold, lifting a mass of snowy blossom to the sun.

Pablo Iballo lifted the figure of his bride from the car, and, without giving her a chance to speak, carried her indoors. He took her up a wide staircase into a magnificent room — a bridal room, full of flowers — with walls panelled in satin, with delicately carved furniture, wide windows, curtained with amber satin, overlooking the mountains and the lake.

Iballo set the trembling girl on her feet. He unhooked his sword and laid it on a chair. Then he put one hand on his hip and smiled at her.

'Will you not unveil for me, *my wife?*' he said.

Even in this panic-stricken moment, Rosemary could not deny that the man was marvellously handsome. Yet his good looks, the very charm of his smile, enraged her.

She flung back the heavy lace veil at last.

'I'm not Mercedes,' she cried breathlessly. 'I've tricked you. You can see — who I am!'

Silence. Paul's dark eyes narrowed to slits. Rosemary shook off her wreath of pearls and orange flowers. Some of the white petals lingered, like snow, in the silver-gilt of her hair.

'It was infamous that Mercedes should be made to marry you,' she added. 'She was terribly in love with someone else. So I helped her to go to him, and went to the Church in her place. Of course the marriage wasn't legal. It can be annulled at once. I'll go now, immediately . . . and you can take what steps you like.'

Another silence. Rosemary's hazel eyes blazed up at Paul. Why didn't he speak? And he was actually smiling. That terrified her. She had expected passionate denunciation, not smiles.

Then he spoke.

'Why did you do this?' he asked quite quietly.

'To help Mercedes.'

'Any other reason?'

'Yes,' she said, her face as white as her dress, her slender body quivering. 'Because I hate you. I wanted to hurt you. I hope I have.'

'But how charming . . . ' His lips continued to smile, but his dark eyes frightened her — they smouldered so.

91

'Yet in the train you didn't hate me — did you?'

'Cad!' she blazed at him. 'No, I didn't hate you then. I didn't know you. I didn't realise that you were engaged to be married ... and just amusing yourself with me. Well, it's my turn to laugh this morning.'

'I should adore to hear you laugh — it would be a pretty sound,' he said.

She stared at him, her brows knit.

'Well — what are you going to do?'

'What should a bridegroom do — but be charming and attentive to his bride?'

His mocking voice infuriated her.

'I'm not your bride. You married me thinking I was Mercedes. The ceremony wasn't legal.'

'I beg your pardon,' said Paul. 'Such a ceremony is quite legal, providing both parties realise whom they are marrying.'

'But *you* didn't know.'

'Your pardon again. I *did* know.'

She stared at him.

92

'You *knew* . . . I was Rosemary?'

'Yes. When I took your hand. Mercedes has very pointed fingers. Yours are pretty, but capable. I know how capable . . . ' He laughed hardly and pointed to his lip. 'When you struck that blow you hurt, you little spitfire.'

'You knew . . . I was Rosemary . . . and married me . . . just the same,' she stammered, face and throat crimson.

'I did. Therefore our marriage, Rose-Marie, is legal and binding, and *you are my wife*!'

The room seemed to spin round her. She caught her heel in her train, and would have fallen, but Paul sprang to her and took her in his arms.

'It's a bridegroom's privilege to support his bride.'

'You're a fiend,' she gasped. 'A devil. You can't say I am your wife . . . I'm not.'

'But you are, Rose-Marie. And I intend to keep you here in my villa . . . for our honeymoon . . . ' His voice vibrated suddenly into such passion that she was rendered speechless, helpless, lying against him in her bridal finery. 'In the train we were young lovers . . . but tonight we'll recapture that spirit and fan it into a fiercer flame . . . I will teach you what love can really be.'

'No!' said Rosemary. 'You're crazy . . . you can't want to keep me here.'

'But I do,' he said. 'It will amuse me to be lover as well as husband to you, darling . . . and the loss of Mercedes affects me not at all. Won't you kiss me . . . as you did in the train?'

'No; let me go. I hate you — and you don't love me.'

'Love doesn't come into this,' said Paul. 'You tried to cheat me — to trick me — you said this was your turn to laugh. But you're wrong, Rose-Marie. It's *my* turn to laugh . . . kiss me . . . go on, *querida* . . . *kiss me*!'

Rosemary hung back in his arms. She tried to speak to him again, and no words came. She tried to evade his kisses, but she was helpless. His arms crushed her against him. She saw his eyes, brilliant, mocking . . . his face, pale with passion, draw nearer to hers. Then she felt on her mouth the fierce pressure of lips that knew no mercy, and gave no respite.

Again and again he kissed her till her very senses seemed to swim. Limp and powerless she lay against him. Darkness seemed to close about her. She was filled with unspeakable terror. She had cheated Don Pablo . . . taken the place of Mercedes and thought she could get away with it. In her wildest moments she had not dreamed that Paul would discover the trick *before* the marriage and continue with it. But that was what he had done. So they had both contracted marriage voluntarily, and that legalised the whole thing.

'I'm his wife,' Rosemary thought in speechless dismay. 'His *wife* . . . and he's going to punish me by keeping me here . . . My God, what a fool I've been.'

A fool indeed. Mad to have done such a crazy thing. What on earth would Ida Bryant say if she knew! Hadn't she always warned Rosemary that she was too impulsive. And it was too late to regret it, or wish she had let Mercedes go to her wedding and work out her own salvation.

The laugh was on the other side. Pablo Iballo held her in the hollow of his hand.

She felt his burning caresses on her eyes, her cheeks, her throat, her hair. Heard his low, husky voice against her ear:

'I have a lovely little wife, most beautiful madonna of the train, with your blonde hair and your golden eyes. Won't you kiss your husband and tell him you love him as much as he loves you?'

Rosemary gasped.

'Love . . . it isn't love to . . . do . . . do this. Brute . . . cad . . . I hate you.'

He laughed, and closed her quivering lips with another fierce kiss.

'It was you, my dear, who have been the little 'brute' to try and cheat me of my wife.'

'You don't love Mercedes.'

'We had better not speak of love, perhaps, only of passion, my little Rose-Marie. That will do for to-night . . . '

His voice sank to a whisper. Then, when he read the shame in those 'golden' eyes, his mood changed. He swung from passion to quiet anger. He lifted her wholly in his arms and carried her to the bed. It was a great four-poster Spanish thing which had once stood in a king's palace. It had a pale yellow canopy of silk and a spread of cloth of gold, marvellously embroidered with the coat of arms of the Iballos at each corner.

Paul laid Rosemary down amongst great satin pillows. The luxury of this villa of his was fantastic. Everything was rich and rare and lovely. Against the satin pillows, Rosemary's face was colourless, but her head was golden as the rich canopy, and her eyes had never looked lovelier. The man looked down at her almost bitterly.

'Stay there, my Rose-Marie, until you've recovered yourself,' he said. 'I'm going into my room to get out of this heavy uniform. Don't humiliate yourself before any of my servants by trying to escape. I have a personal guard in whom I place implicit trust. They have been told that my wife, the Doña Mercedes Iballo, may not leave Villa Lucia or the grounds.'

Rosemary looked up at him, her breath coming with difficulty. This man looked like a prince, behaved like one, a spoiled arrogant prince of wealth, of colossal Spanish pride. And he could keep her here — a prisoner. What hope, therefore, had she of escape?

He took one of her shaking slender hands and kissed it, smiled at her. Don Pablo was heartbreakingly handsome when his cruel mouth softened into such a smile. He said:

'It's a glorious day, sweet. It shall be spent in showing you the beauties of

Villa Lucia. Mercedes' trunks are here. She's gone, I presume, to her violinist. Well, you might as well wear her lovely frocks and look lovelier than she could ever be. Later, when you feel better, I'll come back for you. Our wedding-breakfast will be ready.'

Then he was gone. Rosemary was alone, breathless, dumbfounded by the turn events had taken. She was Don Pablo's legal wife . . . and his prisoner. Rosemary Wallace . . . prisoner of the man who had taught her the meaning of the most intense and passionate love in the Madrid express.

To-day she was definitely afraid of him — even of his physical beauty, his strange fascination. Afraid . . . and conscious of growing dislike. Rosemary was no coward. She had pride, and to be so humiliated by this man made her writhe.

Her door opened. She sat up in the great golden bed, from which she could see the shimmering turquoise sea, every nerve quivering. But it was not Paul. It was a dark-eyed Spanish maid, who curtseyed to her, and said:

'If the Doña Mercedes Iballo is ready, I will help her dress.'

Rosemary had no wish to show this little servant the despair that she was feeling, so she answered with as much calm as she could muster, and allowed one of Mercedes' trunks to be unpacked. The heavy satin bridal robes were laid aside, and the maid, who gave her name as Carmenita dressed Rosemary for her wedding-breakfast.

The rest of the day passed like a dream for Rosemary. A terrifying, exciting dream ... full of fantastic beauty, and yet shadowed with disaster. Don Pablo conducted himself as though he were in truth an adoring bridegroom. If Rosemary remained silent, even sullen, he took no notice of the fact. He strolled with her through gardens of such beauty that she could not help admiring them, even in the midst of her fear. Gardens that had no relation to turbulent human passions, they were so full of quiet serenity. Exquisite flowers, dark, graceful palms; delicately wrought iron gateways through which one looked, down avenues of slim trees and roses, to white fountains — to lily ponds. Terrace after terrace, down the mountain-side to the shimmering sea.

Inside the villa everything was magnificent . . . the old Spanish walnut furniture, the tapestried walls, rare paintings of Velasquez, and fine old glass and painted china.

★　★　★

Later, when the sun dipped into the sea and the stars and moon came out, flooding the mountains with silver, investing it with almost unearthly splendour, Paul sat at a table in the garden, where it was warm and perfumed, and dined with his bride. A wonderful dinner, served by liveried men . . . choicest wines . . . most delicate food . . . lamps hung from the trees, and tall wax candles flickering on the table.

Across that flower-decked table, Paul's handsome face was a brown mask, whilst his eyes smiled at Rosemary and mocked her. She sat like a figure carved of stone; but lovelier than she had ever looked in her life, in one of Mercedes' trousseau gowns — white chiffon, which befitted a bride — little white satin shoes, and a diamond necklace about her throat, glittering fire in the candlelight. Paul had clasped jewels about the slender neck just before they dined.

'They are the Iballo diamonds . . . and have hung around no more exquisite throat,' he had said carelessly, then kissed her just where the sapphire clasp touched the nape of her neck. She had shivered uncontrollably.

She was hating him to-night, yet the touch of his lips brought back poignant memories of those hours in the train when she had fallen in love with him . . . memories which hurt all the more acutely because she believed that the brief ecstasy of loving Paul had died — had been killed stone dead by him and his treatment of her.

Several times during that day she had tried to escape. Several times she had walked by herself through the grounds. And, when she reached the gateways leading out to the road, she met with a barrier in the form of Paul's men. Spaniards who treated her with infinite courtesy and respect but barred her progress.

'Your pardon, Doña Mercedes ... but, by orders, no one may leave Villa Lucia to-day. It is not safe. There is news of mountain robbers who have come down to the district.'

Always a polite, and quite impossible story of that kind ... one that Rosemary knew to be childish and untrue. But she could see Paul's power in his own domain. No one would dare disobey his orders. Indeed none of his servants wished to disobey. They appeared to worship him. Rosemary, furious, impotent, had had no choice but to turn and walk back to the villa, where Paul met her. He said nothing, but his splendid eyes silently laughed at her chagrin.

Now, to-night, leaving the meal half tasted, Rosemary told herself that this thing could not continue. It was ridiculous — just like an absurd film story, the sort of wild romance which she and Ida used to laugh at in London cinemas. When the servants had vanished, she looked across at Paul, impatiently.

'Hasn't this joke gone far enough? Hadn't you better let me go?' she said.

He was smoking a cigar. The fragrant smoke wafted across to her. He wore evening clothes, but, except for his jet-black head and ivory skin, he looked very English . . . with the mark of an English tailor about him. He smiled at her.

'My sweet — you make a mistake. There's no joke about this. You married me this morning . . . Naturally I shall not part from my newly made wife, and the Lamandas fondly imagine Mercedes is up here with me, so they won't interfere — though they may of course wonder what has happened to you.'

She sprang to her feet. In the white chiffon dress, with her pale young face, she looked a pale, sculptured statue. He knew he tormented her. In a queer, vague way he was worried because he hurt her, yet he wanted to go on hurting her. She had dared to trick him . . . to defy him . . . to make him, Pablo Iballo, a laughing-stock.

'I refuse to regard myself as your real wife, Paul,' she said. 'You must be mad to think I shall stay. You can't keep me a prisoner for ever. Such . . . such conduct is *savage*.'

Paul pitched his cigar into the shadows. He rose and walked to her side.

'Perhaps I am savage, sweet,' he said. 'Anyhow, you're in one of the Iballo *haciendas*, and in such I am supreme.'

'If you knew how I hate you!' she

began through clenched teeth.

'I do know. And perhaps I hate you, Rose-Marie, for what you did this morning. But I still . . . want you . . . '

His voice sank. With a swift gesture he had her in his arms.

'No,' she said breathlessly. 'Paul, please . . . you can't mean . . . you mustn't . . . '

'The word 'mustn't' doesn't exist for me in Villa Lucia, Rose-Marie, and I always mean what I say. Don't struggle, don't cry. Just rest in my arms and admit you're beaten.'

'I'm not beaten . . . you shan't say that.'

He shrugged his shoulders. In the train she had been sweet . . . unforgettable. Well, he had deliberately made her his wife. Mercedes Lamanda was nothing to him . . . never had meant much. And, now that the promise to his father was broken, nothing else mattered. Rosemary was his wife, and nothing, he told himself, on earth or in heaven should take her from him now.

The passionate heart of the man was a raging furnace of conflicting emotions — of stubborn pride and anger and desire, of a queer longing to conquer this girl . . . to make her admit that she was still in love with him.

'I shall never let you go, Rose-Marie,' he said. '*Never*; whatever happens now. We're married . . . there's a bond between us that nothing can dissolve.'

'If I had known,' she said. 'Oh, if only I'd known you were going to do this.'

'Quite; you expected to get out of it lightly. But there's nothing light about it, Rose-Marie. You've taken me . . . for better . . . for worse. And to-night I claim what belongs to me.'

'No,' she said. 'No.'

'Be a little kind, sweet,' he said in a caressing voice. 'I've led a wild, lonely life. My beautiful villa here in Malaga has needed you only to make it a paradise. There are thousands of stars shining for us. Let us be the lovers of the Madrid express once more. Come, sweet . . . let us talk of love and forget revenge . . . '

He lifted her right up in his strong arms. Pausing by the table, he blew out the candles, one by one. She lay against him in a kind of stupor . . . her heart-beats suffocating her. She did not know what she felt in this instant . . . wild longing for his tenderness . . . or wild hatred because he was breaking her to his will. But she felt the ruthless passion of his lips against her mouth as he carried her through the moonlit garden into the villa and up to their room.

She seemed to see nothing but flowers — fragrant white blossoms, strewn on the floor of their bridal suite . . . masses of golden roses covering the great four-poster bed. The romantic Spanish servants had done all this for their adored master and his bride.

Don Pablo laid Rosemary down amongst the roses. Her heart thudded violently. Her eyes asked him dumbly for the mercy she knew he would not show. He lifted a handful of the bruised yellow petals and scattered them over her white gown and her golden hair.

'*Alma de mi vida*,' he said. 'Let's forget our differences. I can only remember that you loved me once . . . and that my heart is on fire for you . . . to-night.'

He crushed her, roses and all, in his arms, and silenced her little broken cry with his kisses.

3

Four days went by. Four days — four nights since Rosemary Wallace became the Iballo's wife in Mercedes' place. Days and nights of strain — of conflict, mental and physical — of intolerable humiliation for her, of conquest for him.

She seemed to be completely shut away from her old world. She lived in a new, strange one which had no connection with the last. She had no communication outside Villa Lucia. Only the letters she wrote to her friend in London were posted. Paul allowed her that, and Rosemary had written to tell Ida Bryant of her sudden marriage. She could barely imagine Ida's horror and consternation.

Time taught Rosemary that it was futile for her to try to get away. Every effort only added to her humiliation. So finally she ceased to try. But she knew that one day, when the chance came, she would take it.

Every kiss Paul burned upon her lips burned itself on her very soul. She hated him, she told herself. He was cruel and remorseless. Yet as a lover he was perfect . . . and all that he did or said when she was in his arms seemed touched by beauty . . . a beauty almost heartbreaking. She felt that he had long since broken her heart, and that only her body remained his prisoner. And always at the back of her mind lay the anguished reflection that, had she met and loved Paul under different circumstances, she might have been wildly happy as his wife. There was just that charm about the man that nobody could deny.

The Lamandas had by now, of course, discovered that their daughter had tricked them, aided and abetted by her English companion. Outraged, furious, they had come to Villa Lucia to demand an explanation, only to be told that Don Pablo sent his regrets. Mercedes had chosen Manuel Cadozza, and since Miss Wallace had taken her place, he, Iballo, had decided to leave things as they were. He had hoped to keep his promise to his father, but, now that things had happened like this, he would lead his own life and choose his own pathway.

So the scandal spread round Malaga of the amazing marriage. The Lamandas fretted and fumed helplessly. Mercedes had vanished to Barcelona with her young lover, and Rosemary, who had in a crazy moment instigated the whole business, went through her punishment in shame and bitterness.

Again and again she cried to Paul:

'Let me go . . . '

And every time he held her close, and, between those slow, remorseless kisses of his, whispered:

'Never, my sweet. You're my wife, and I shall never let you go.'

Then a visitor came to Villa Lucia. An unexpected visitor, to whom Don

Pablo did not refuse admittance. An Englishman, from London, by name Harry Dyall, and first cousin to Paul, whose mother had been half English.

When a servant announced that the English señor had arrived in his car, on his way through Spain, Paul told Rosemary that she must receive Harry Dyall kindly and entertain him.

'He's my cousin and my friend, and was, until four days ago, the heir to the Iballo fortune, should I die.'

Rosemary gave him a cold look. 'Is he no longer the heir, then?'

'No,' said Paul. 'I hope for a son.'

Rosemary went scarlet to the roots of her lovely hair.

'I hate you,' she said.

Those were the first words Harry Dyall heard his cousin's wife utter as he entered the long cool *salon* wherein they received him.

He heard with interest. Outwardly he was a well-groomed, typical looking Englishman, with brown hair and blue eyes . . . the antithesis of Paul, who had inherited his Spanish father's dark, foreign beauty. Inwardly he was a furnace of anger and disappointment.

When Harry Dyall had arrived at Villa Lucia and heard that his cousin, Don Pablo, was with the Doña Mercedes, he had grit his teeth with rage. He was next of kin to Paul. Paul who had been at school with him and liked him — supplied him with a good deal of money. The marriage would spoil everything. Paul would grow mean, want his riches for himself and his bride, and he would possibly have a son. Harry Dyall was a pleasant, easy-going young man to meet, but he was a weak character and utterly lacking in scruples.

He was first of all astonished, then intrigued, when he heard a soft, girlish voice say, 'I hate you.' So Paul's new wife was not madly in love? That was better. Harry took a look at the slim young woman in pearl grey georgette with a long necklace of jade about her white throat, and he was more than ever intrigued. Paul's wife was English — beautiful and charming.

Harry bowed, and murmured suave congratulations over Rosemary's hand. She received them quietly. But she had already made up her mind that Paul's cousin, Harry, would be the means of her escape. He was her countryman. His blue eyes rested upon her a trifle boldly, perhaps, but she took no notice of that. She wanted a friend, and she was ready to look upon the first stranger who came to Villa Lucia as such.

'I did not dream you were married, old man,' Harry Dyall said. 'I won't stay of course . . . '

'But do stay — please — we should be delighted,' came from Rosemary quickly.

Harry cast her a questioning look. He could read some queer distress in her golden eyes. He wondered what was wrong here. He wondered, also, how Paul had come to marry an English woman. Harry had heard, in England, that Paul was engaged to a Spanish girl.

Paul walked to his wife's side. He put an arm about her.

'Rose-Marie and I are in the midst of honeymooning,' he said, smiling. 'But of course . . . stay a few days, Harry.'

His arm was a band of steel about Rosemary's shoulders. She shivered and bit her lip. Harry saw the colour that dyed her face and throat. He meant to investigate the matter.

He heard the story of Paul's marriage from both sides. Paul, himself, confided in his cousin:

'I want it kept entirely secret, Harry,' he said seriously. 'Rose-Marie and I are married, and as such we are going to remain. I have had my fling. I would like to settle down now . . . with my wife and — children.'

Harry said nothing. His moody eyes looked at Paul without much liking. He was irritated by the splendid good looks, the vitality, of his Spanish cousin. Harry himself was always hard up.

Keen on women, on wine, on horse-racing, he was generally in debt. He would very much like to have Paul's money. It maddened him to think that all this would pass if Paul 'settled down'.

There was something else he wanted now. Paul's wife. Harry, always susceptible to a pretty woman, had decided that he had never seen anything quite so bewitching as Rosemary. She fired his imagination. He pictured himself with Paul's money as well as Paul's wife until the vision tormented him.

He shook Paul warmly by the hand, and assured him of his loyalty and approval.

'Whatever you do is right, old man,' he said in his hypocritical fashion. 'And the girl deserves to be punished for that rotten trick she tried to play on you.'

Paul tried to bask in the sunshine of Harry's sympathy. But in his heart of heart he was never quite sure that he was doing the right thing. And when he held his wife in his arms, and felt her tremble under his hot kisses, all that was best and most chivalrous in him wanted to let her go free . . . to be kind to her. But passion and the obstinate wish to punish her won the battle between good and evil in Pablo Iballo — for the time being.

The other side of the story was poured into Harry Dyall's ears by Paul's wife, later that evening.

They had all three dined together in the magnificent dining-hall with its painted ceiling and old Flemish tapestries, and then Paul disappeared to his writing-room and left his cousin and his wife alone.

Harry, only too pleased to have a tête-à-tête with Doña Rosemary Iballo, strolled with her into the starlit gardens.

She was as lovely as a picture, he thought, with her shining head, her graceful figure, her hazel shadowy eyes. She wore black chiffon and pearls to-night. Her face looked pale and strained.

Harry said: 'Tell me what is troubling

you, little cousin Rosemary.'

He won her confidence, and, half in tears, she told him exactly what had happened between her and Paul.

'Mercedes hated him. She loved another man . . . and he had played a cruel game with me . . . I did not see why he should get it all his own way. I admit it was wrong. But why should he keep me here now?'

Harry looked at her strangely.

'Do you want very much to get away?'

'I want nothing else.'

'My cousin is a cad,' said Harry softly. 'He has no right to treat you in this way.'

Rosemary's spirits rose.

'Then you are on my side, Mr. Dyall?'

'I am your first cousin by marriage. Won't you call me 'Harry'?' he said. 'And look on me as your friend. Yes, of course I am on your side — absolutely. I think Paul is mad. He always was a bit crazy — even at school we thought so.

He used to do crazy things and break all the damned rules.'

She looked at Harry mournfully. He looked kindness itself. She put out a hand, and he patted it as though he were a brother. He did not betray the sudden desire in him, which was to sweep that beautiful young figure into his arms.

'Trust me,' he murmured. 'Rely on me. You want to get away from Villa Lucia?'

'Yes, yes. Oh, will you help me ... will you?'

'I will,' he nodded slowly. 'Yes, my dear, I will.'

And through his quick brain there leapt many interesting and exciting thoughts. He would be only too pleased to separate Paul from his wife and put an end to their farce of a honeymoon. He did not want Paul to settle down to marriage, neither did Harry intend that Paul should have an heir and disinherit him in consequence. Yes, gladly he would take Rosemary away.

She placed her entire faith and trust in him that night, and when Paul joined them in the garden, five minutes later, she was smiling. She looked under her long lashes at the handsome, ruthless face of her husband, and her pulse raced as she said to herself:

'And now, Paul, we shall see which one of us is going to win the final victory.'

★ ★ ★

They sat up till late in the magnificent library of the Villa Lucia. The cousins smoked and talked and drank whiskies-and-sodas in British fashion. Rosemary sat silent, watching, listening, looking from one man to the other. Against her will she had to admit that Paul was the handsomer, the most attractive, of the two. But she had to shut her heart against him. He was a brute to her, and she hated him. She was going to run away from him — with Harry Dyall.

Every now and then Paul's eyes

turned to her. What she read in them made the colour scorch her face and throat, and she grew paler than before. She knew exactly what to expect. Every night, since their amazing marriage, he opened the door for her to pass through on her way to her room, bent as she passed, kissed her shoulder, whispered:

'Sweet — my lady Iballo — in a few minutes I shall be with you.'

And she was powerless to fight him. There was not even a key to her door. He had taken that.

She was so utterly humiliated that she was blinded now with exaggerated dislike and fear of him. With fear of herself too, because she was not an ice-cold, marble creature without feeling. And at moments in his arms, with his brown passionate face so close to hers and his heart pounding against her own, she found it difficult to resist him, or forget the rapture of their journey to Madrid. And that very difficulty made her all the more furious with him and with herself; all the more anxious to get away from him.

In a feverish way she looked upon Harry Dyall as her saviour. In his blue eyes she read only friendliness and the desire to help her, and knew nothing of the treachery in the man's heart.

She rose, at last, and said coldly: 'Forgive me if I go to bed. I am tired.' To herself she thought: 'If Paul looks at me, I'll give no sign that I understand or care . . . '

But as she stood there, her heart racing, she felt her eyes drawn to him. Yes, he was smiling very slightly. The darkness of his eyes held and magnetised her. Against her whole will, she blushed fiery red. She walked out of the library without another word, her fair young head flung back defiantly. But she could feel his expressive gaze following her, and knew that her burning colour had given her away. She felt furious with herself.

Harry Dyall had also seen that blush. He thought it was sheer anger. He also thought what an intriguing thing it would be if he could make Rosemary colour for a different reason, if only a man could kiss that glorious red into her cheeks and throat.

He would find it very easy to fall in love with his cousin's wife. Almost as much as he was in love with Paul's money and this exquisite *hacienda* in Spain. He would like them all — yes, why should Paul have everything, damn him?

Paul, seated again, poured out another small drink in a fine crystal goblet. Harry was about to sit down when he noticed a tiny wisp of black chiffon on the polished floor. He stooped and picked it up. It was a ridiculous, gossamer handkerchief. It smelt of flowers . . . some favourite scent that Rosemary used. Harry Dyall's pulse leaped curiously. He turned to his cousin:

'Your wife has dropped her handkerchief, old man. One moment . . . I'll give it to her.'

Paul smiled and nodded. There were

no suspicions in his mind.

Harry hastened into the wide hall. Rosemary was mounting the staircase, slowly, as though very tired. She saw Harry cross to the foot of the stairs, and paused. In her long black dress, she was a lovely, regal young figure, standing beside a long, low window that looked out over the starlit gardens. Harry Dyall sprang up the stairs two at a time. He reached her side, and pressed the chiffon scented handkerchief into her hand.

'You dropped this. Listen . . . I know you are terribly unhappy. I am sorry for you, my dear.'

His sympathy was like honey to her. Swift tears sprang to her eyes. She said under her breath: 'Oh, yes . . . please, cousin Harry, help me to get away.'

'To-morrow,' he said.

'When?'

'Before the others in the villa are awake. I have a plan. I am going to tell Paul to-night that I must be on my way to Granada early to-morrow morning, and will motor away before breakfast. You, of course, will go with me. But, when we are right away, I shall telephone to the villa, and say that I have just seen you in Malaga, and was so amazed I had to phone up and ask if anything was wrong. Then Paul won't think I have helped you. I don't want him to connect us at all.'

That seemed to Rosemary quite sound. She nodded eagerly.

'Yes, very well. I will creep away . . . about half past five . . . I will be down here at the front door.'

'You will trust me?' said Harry with his hypocritical smile.

She gave him a hand, and whispered: 'Yes, I must . . . I do . . . '

He wanted to cover the small, tapering fingers with kisses, but dared not. So he just pressed her hand and walked away. She went on up to her room.

The little Spanish maid, Carmenita, was there to help her to undress, put plenty of sweet-smelling salts in the green marble sunken bath, which was one of the villa's greatest luxuries, then brush the señora's lovely hair until it shone and rippled like gold.

Half an hour later, Don Pablo entered his wife's room.

She was standing on the balcony that looked down the mountain-side toward the sea. A full moon shone on her. In her white velvet wrapper, folded over a nightgown of pale pink satin which had been made for Mercedes' trousseau, Rosemary was so lovely that for the moment Paul stood spellbound, gazing at her.

All the fierce passion and unrest in his heart culminated into a tremendous desire to revive the tenderness, the mutual rapture, of their first embraces and caresses in the Madrid express.

He knew he had won a battle over her in a physical sense, but that her mind, her heart, were shut to him, and that she hated him. The magic of the moonlight over the perfect gardens, and of her own beautiful young figure, shook him to the depths.

He crossed swiftly to her side, put out a hand and caught her arm, drew her from the balcony into the dim, lamp-lit room. Just one light in a Moorish lamp swinging over the great golden bed.

He said, close to her ear:

'How lovely you are . . . Rose-Marie, my Rose-Marie. I'm rather sick of this one-sided passion and all your coldness and your tears. Once you trembled in my arms. Can you not tremble again? Sweet, let's forget the past. To-night let's be perfect lovers. We were made for each other, you and I!'

Rosemary stood very still in the circle of his arms. Still and cold. But her pulse fluttered in a queer wild way. How handsome he was . . . fresh from his bath . . . jet black hair curving back from his fine forehead . . . glistening like a raven's wing . . . dark eyes half shut, dreamy, entreating. She could see the pulse in his throat beating, for her. The tall, splendid figure in the rich satin dressing-gown of tulip-red, was shaking for her. Yes, she *had* trembled in his arms in that train, weeks ago. If she let her pride go now . . . let body and brain relax . . . she could tremble again. She could easily fling her arms about his neck and say:

'I love you . . . Paul. Paul, I am all yours . . . '

But she stood still, white as her velvet wrap, her passions in leash, proud, contemptuous of him. She said:

'You must be a fool to imagine I could love you again after all you've done to me. You had no right to keep me here — to make me stay as your wife. I shall never forgive it.'

'But wait, Rose-Marie.' He flung back his handsome head with a gesture of impatience. 'I, also, might say you behaved unforgivably in the way you tricked me . . . in the way you would have made me a laughing-stock for my friends when you took Mercedes' place that day.'

'I admit I did wrong. But you

deserved it. You made love to me in the train, knowing that you were engaged to Mercedes. Why?'

He looked away from her.

'I chose to . . . forget Mercedes for a few hours.'

'That was nice for me!' she sneered.

'I was sorry for it,' he admitted, stung by her accusations. 'But in any case it couldn't justify what you did to me.'

She pressed both hands against her tired eyes.

'I don't see the use of going on like this. We only loathe each other.'

Then his mood changed, and he took her back in his arms, and pressed his hot lips against both the small cold hands.

'That isn't quite true, Rose-Marie. We don't really loathe each other. We're both angry . . . but anger is such a part of love . . . this sort of love.'

For an instant she looked up at him as though about to say something bitter and furious. Then she desisted. What was the use of arguing with him? He was adamant, and she had made her plans to leave him, to go away with Harry Dyall. This was the last night she would ever have to spend with Paul. The final humiliation.

When she felt his lips against the corner of her mouth, she shivered uncontrollably. He whispered:

'Kiss me, love me, Rose-Marie . . . '

But there was no warmth, no response, from her. And she hated more than loved him because he was so much the stronger of the two and she could do nothing but lie helplessly in his arms and accept the caresses he poured upon her.

She told herself:

'This is the last time. This is good-bye, if you only knew it, Paul. To-morrow I shall be gone, and this farce will be ended at last.'

4

Dawn came — a wonderful dawn. The sky a haze of pearl and pink, the mountain peaks hidden in the mist. The garden like a green shell, mysterious, full of secret beauty. And Paul's white *hacienda* silent and lovely amid the flowers.

Noiselessly, with utmost care, Rosemary left her husband's side, and managed to dress herself without waking him. The shutters were still drawn and the room was dim. Paul, one arm behind his dark head, slept the healthy, dreamless slumber of youth. Just before Rosemary gathered a few things together in a suitcase and tip-toed from the room, she paused beside the bed, to glance at him.

How young, how beautiful, he was in his sleep. The cruelty, the egotism, wiped from his face. She told herself that she hated him. Yet a pang rent her when she took this, her final look at him. A pang for the might-have-been: for the Paul she had first loved; for the early rapture that had died through his callousness.

She told herself that she never wished to set eyes on him or the Villa Lucia again. Noiselessly she slipped down to the hall. She found Harry Dyall, wearing a coat, muffler, and cap, pacing up and down the marble hall.

His eyes glistened when he saw the slim girl steal down the wide staircase toward him. She looked about seventeen in her blue and grey tweeds, and that beret set carelessly on the fair curls.

'Good for you,' he whispered. 'Come along quickly. First to the garage . . . for my car.'

'We aren't safe yet. Paul has me watched . . . even at night. There are men on duty at the main gate.'

Harry's lips twisted.

'I'll fix them. Don't worry. You shan't

be kept here against your will any longer. Look here . . . as soon as we get to my car I shall put you in the back and cover you with rugs. You must lie down on the floor until we are past the guards. Then nobody will know . . . no one will question my right to get away. Do you see?'

'Yes, I see,' she nodded. 'Quickly, then.'

There was nothing but rejoicing in her heart when finally they were in Henry's big Bugatti moving through the gateway out of the grounds of the villa. A sleepy man on duty took a look at the car, saw only the Englishman at the wheel, and the luggage on the grid, and said, in Spanish: *'Bueno!'*

Rosemary crouched motionless under the rugs. The car seemed to travel some distance. Then it stopped. A hand drew the rugs from her. She sat up, flushed and hot, to find herself over two miles away from Villa Lucia on the curving, tortuous road leading across the mountainside to Granada. Harry Dyall smiled at her, his eyes victorious.

'Wasn't that well done?'

'Marvellous.'

'Come and sit beside me now.'

She stepped into the seat beside him. He gave her an intent look. She was charming in her tweeds, he thought. She looked thoroughbred. She would be a pleasant and attractive companion for his travels through Spain. They were well away from Paul, and serve him right. He detested his cousin, Don Pablo.

Rosemary looked around her, then stretched out her arms. She sighed.

'Free!' she whispered. 'Am I really free?'

'Absolutely,' said Harry.

But he did not intend that she should continue into freedom alone. He had taken her from Paul's prison, but he hoped to put her into his own.

Rosemary thought of Villa Lucia, of Paul waking in the first beam of sunlight to find her gone. She shivered suddenly. A little thrill of fear shot through her . . . when she pictured what he might do — what might happen if he followed and found her again. She clutched Harry Dyall's arm.

'Oh, quickly,' she said. 'Let's get on.'

'You needn't be afraid,' he said. 'I'll look after you, Rosemary.'

'Where are we going?'

'To a place I know between here and Granada. There is a village . . . Molinos, where wine is made . . . it is full of vineyards. I had a room there once in an old inn — the Fonda — on a tour. No one would dream of looking there. I'll take you there.'

Rosemary was satisfied.

'And then to-morrow we can get on to Granada, and I must make arrangements for my return to England,' she said.

'Quite so,' was Harry's reply.

So she drove with him through the fresh dawn to Molinos. They left the outskirts of Malaga behind them. Villa Lucia seemed to fade and become an unreal dream, Rosemary felt, like her marriage to Don Pablo.

They reached the vineyards of Molinos at ten o'clock, after four and a half hours' driving.

The Fonda, to which Harry took Rosemary, was a whitewashed inn with green shutters, and a tangled garden, overlooking hot, sunlit vineyards. A lonely place half a mile from the village. The owners were Spanish peasants, an old man with a brown wrinkled face, and his wife, Maria, fat, still handsome, and typical of the country.

They did not speak the pure Castilian Spanish which Rosemary understood, only a patois. But Harry, clever with languages, made himself understood.

They sat out in the garden under a canopy of flowering creeper, which formed a shade from the sun. And Maria served them with hot coffee and omelettes.

Harry ate hungrily, but Rosemary had little appetite. She sipped the coffee in miserable silence, trying to make up her mind that she was glad that she had escaped from Paul. But she could not help thinking about him and wondering how he would be affected by her escape, and whether she would ever see him again in this world.

Her gratitude to Harry was a little shadowed by a feeling of uneasiness. She was not altogether sure that she liked Paul's cousin. He had a furtive way of looking at her, and refusing to meet her full in the eyes. And, now that the first thrill of the escape was over, it struck her suddenly that she was in a bad position with this man. She had no money. Paul had given her everything that she wanted . . . except hard cash. Maybe he had anticipated that she would attempt an escape, and that was why he had refused her money.

She had to rely on 'cousin Harry' entirely.

When the meal was finished, Harry offered her a cigarette.

'No thanks,' she said.

'Cheer up. You ought to be in the

best of spirits. We're well away.'

'Oh, yes!' Rosemary tried to laugh. 'It's been just like a film, hasn't it? Wife escapes from husband over the mountains, etc., etc.'

'Well.' Harry smoked his own cigarette, looking at Rosemary's fair, haunting face through a cloud of smoke. 'Now we must make our plans for the future.'

'I've got to get back to London, and I'm afraid it means that I've got to borrow the wherewithal from you.'

'Easy, in spite of the fact that cousin Harry has the reputation for being permanently broke. But I made a few hundred this last month by backing a big winner at the races. I'm quite willing to play fairy god-father, cousin Rosemary. But what are you going to do for me in return?'

Rosemary gave him a sharp look. She knew enough about men and the world by now to read what lay in those rather indolent blue eyes of Harry Dyall's. And she did not like what she saw. She sighed a little wearily to herself. Must there always be a payment ... for everything? And, having escaped from Paul, was there going to be an emotional disturbance with Harry? She was tired to death of the passions of men.

'There isn't much I can do for you,' she said, 'except get a job as soon as I'm home, and pay you back bit by bit.'

'Quite unnecesary. Now I have another suggestion. I want to see a bit more of Spain before I return to London. How about coming with me? I've got a nice car, haven't I? And we could have a swell time together, and ...'

'Of course you're talking nonsense,' she broke in, and stood up.

He came close to her.

'It isn't nonsense. I mean it. Come along with me for a few weeks, Rosemary, and then we'll drive back through France, homewards. It's as good a way as any of getting back to the old country, and more amusing for you than if you rushed back alone and without a sou.'

She looked up at him, her lips hard and unsmiling. 'This isn't very honourable of you, Harry.'

He shrugged his shoulders. 'My darling girl, honour was never my strong point.'

'You said that you'd help me, and that's why I came with you.'

'Aren't I offering to? It's only a question of the *way* you get home.'

'Well, I don't fancy your way, Harry. And I'm not accepting it.'

He put his tongue in his cheek. 'So particular? The girl who takes another woman's place and traps a wealthy young Spaniard into matrimony?'

She flushed scarlet. Her heart throbbed uneasily. This escape wasn't turning out in the least the way she had meant it to. She felt more than disappointed. She felt trapped. If this was what Harry had at the back of his head, it was going to make things impossible for her. Naturally the idea of going along with Harry in the way he suggested was out of the question. And now that he had made such a suggestion it put her in a very invidious position.

She gave him a long look. She was beginning to see the lines of weakness and dissipation in his face. He presented himself in his true colours now. He was a despicable character. If he would stoop to this, there was no knowing what else he might do. She was surprised that Paul had never seen through him. But of course he had always been delightful to Paul . . . he knew which side his bread was buttered.

'Harry,' at length she said. 'I don't think this is the time or the place to remind me of what I did about Paul. You were extremely sympathetic with me at Villa Lucia.'

He caught her hand and squeezed it. 'I'm willing to be even more sympathetic now, my dear.'

She snatched her hand away. 'Oh, don't be so impossible!' she flashed.

The very contact with his fingers infuriated her. She knew that while she lived she would never want another man to touch her. God alone knew the bitter ecstasy that had been hers in Paul's arms! It had been a disaster. But it was the end of love and loving for her.

'Come, Rosemary, be a sport,' Harry said smoothly. 'You hate Paul. So do I.'

'*You* hate him.'

'You don't expect me to love him, do you? He's got everything that I want, and he's determined to have a son and heir which will cut me right out of it. Frankly, I loathe him.'

She looked at him scornfully. Whatever she, personally, felt about Paul, she was contemptuous of his cousin's treachery.

'Aren't you vile, Harry!'

'You've done unprincipled things yourself, my dear.'

'You don't understand . . . there were extenuating circumstances when I married Paul,' she began hotly, then paused, and spread out her hands with a helpless gesture. 'But what's the good of arguing? Don't let's waste time. What do you intend to do? I'm not coming with you . . . in the way you suggest. And obviously I can't stay here in this forsaken village. Well, what about it?'

'I don't know. I'm not keen on helping you for nothing.'

'At least you're frank.'

'Quite. And neither do I want you to go back to Paul.'

'I've no intention of doing that. I don't suppose he'd take me back now, in any case.'

'All the better.'

'Why should it worry you so desperately if I *do* go back?'

'Your intelligence should tell you that. I want to stop any possibility of you presenting Paul with his son and heir.'

Again her cheeks and throat burnt scarlet.

'There won't be any possibility of that,' she said in a low voice.

She looked so lovely with that flaming colour that the man was stirred to passion.

'Lord, but you're lovely, Rose-Marie.'

She stamped her foot.

'Don't dare call me that.'

'Ho! Ho!' he laughed. 'Does that strike a romantic note?'

'Oh, you beast . . . '

He put an arm round her.

'You make me one. I'd much rather be friendly . . . and I could be as romantic a lover as my cousin if I were given the chance. I'm quite mad about you, Rosemary.'

She shook herself out of his embrace. But, before she could speak again, the old innkeeper came out and addressed Harry.

'Señor . . . a big car is coming up the hill, señor.'

Harry left Rosemary's side and walked to the end of the garden. The Fonda was built on the summit of a hill, and from here Harry could see over the vineyards down the valley to the white twisting roadway with its many hairpin bends and fringe of dusty olive-trees. Some miles down a car was climbing the hill. Now and then the bonnet flashed in the sunlight. It took Harry only a second in which to recognise that car. His lips took an unpleasant downward curve. He called Rosemary.

'Come here and look . . . isn't that Paul's Hispano?'

Rosemary's heart missed a beat. Running to Harry's side she shaded her eyes with her hand, looked down the valley, and recognised that familiar car.

'My God! Yes, it is!'

'Clever, isn't he?' said Harry in an ugly voice. 'And now what are we going to do? We musn't be found together. If he thinks I'm eloping with you, he'll chuck me out, and I won't get another penny.'

Rosemary flung him a scornful look.

She did not care what Paul did to Harry. She was only wondering what Paul was going to do *to her*! At least it wouldn't be fair for him to imagine that this escape was in the nature of an elopement.

'Go away,' she told Harry hysterically. 'Go along — get your car and take that other road which leads away from the inn.'

'And what are you going to say to Paul?'

'That I made you take me.'

'He won't believe that.'

'I'll tell him something.'

'Well, make it a credible tale,' said Harry tersely. 'Otherwise he'll take it for granted that we're eloping. Are you sure you won't come with me?'

'No, thanks. I'd rather stay here and face the music.'

His lips curled. 'Be it on your own head, then. But I'm going to see you again one day. This won't be the end.'

'Oh, go!' she said passionately. 'It will ruin us both if we're found together.'

Harry ran into the inn. He spat a few terse orders at the Spaniards, started up his car, and a moment later vanished down the road toward Granada. And from the south came the roar and hum of another big racing-car, advancing nearer, and raising a cloud of white dust as it came.

Rosemary walked into the inn, and stood at the door, waiting. She was sick at heart, and her pulse was racing at a furious pace. Useless to try and escape from Paul. He was too strong, too powerful, for her. And now the green and silver nose of the Hispano glittered in the sunshine. The big wheels scrunched on the road as Don Pablo rounded the last bend and pulled up before the green-shuttered Fonda.

Rosemary shook so that she could scarcely stand as she saw him. Here he was again . . . this tyrant from whom she had fondly imagined she had escaped at dawn.

Paul stepped out of the car and moved toward Rosemary. He was smiling, but he was livid under his tan, and his eyes were bitter and furious. She could not help noticing how handsome, how *soigné*, he was, even after his chase . . . he wore his grey flannels well, and there was just that strange mixture of careless Spanish grace and English reserve about him. He took off his wide-brimmed hat, brushed a black lock of hair back from a wet forehead, and bowed.

'*Buenos!*' he said. 'So you are here, my Doña Rose-Marie. You've given me an exciting chase, although it was a little early for my liking, my sweet.'

Like one rooted to the ground Rosemary stared at him. The familiar voice of the man wakened a thousand memories, fierce, passionate, sad, and, above all, a furious resentment. She flung back her head defiantly.

'You may think you're very clever to have traced me here, Paul, but it isn't difficult, really, for a man with an army of spies to find one defenceless woman.'

Paul laughed. He came closer to her, stared her up and down with frank curiosity.

'You amuse me, beautiful. I must say

you aren't looking as fascinating as usual. You've been crying. But how sad! Your hair is untidy, and your charming nose is pink and shiny. I can hardly bear it. Won't you run up to your room and use a little cream and face-powder and become your exquisite self again? Running away doesn't exactly suit you.'

She gasped. The audacity of this man. His eyes could look so velvety and caressing, his hands and lips could bestow such tenderness . . . and under it all he was iron and steel. What chance had she or any woman against Don Pablo?

'I'm glad you're amused by me,' she said.

'Were you amused to play the faithless wife and steal away with cousin Harry?' he drawled. And then the smile vanished. His lips were a thin line. One slim brown hand shot out and seized her wrist. '*Madre de dios*, Rose-Marie,' he added. 'If you've behaved with Harry as you did with me on the train, I'll *kill* you. It shall never be said that the wife of Don Pablo has fooled him. And Harry — my own kin . . . '

'Don't be ridiculous,' she broke in, flushed and trembling. 'You really needn't be so violent, Paul. I can tell you now, straight away, that I had no intention of 'fooling' with your cousin. I think I had my lesson — in the train!'

Paul drew a deep breath.

'So . . . ' he said.

'And if I *did* choose to elope with your cousin, or with any other man on earth, what right would you have to object? You've only kept me by sheer force,' she added hysterically.

'That may be true, Rose-Marie, but you are my wife. By your own free will you married me.'

'I never meant it.'

'Oh, yes you did, and before God you shall keep to your bargain.'

She swayed, and her eyes closed. She was near to fainting. She felt his arm about her waist. He led her out of the hot sunlight into the shade of the palm-trees close to the little Fonda.

'Where is Harry?' he asked her. 'Tell me the truth.'

With fair hair drooping, she made her explanation.

'I hid in the back of his car — he stopped here for breakfast ... I got out ... he went on without me ... '

Paul watched her intently. He was not sure she was telling him the truth, but he said nothing until she finished her stammered little story. Then he said:

'And on your oath to me, Rose-Marie, you did not strike a bargain with my cousin? You weren't by any chance attracted by him?'

'No, on the contrary, I disliked him. I give you my oath on that, since you choose to be jealous.'

Paul drew another deep breath. For the last few hours he had indeed been tormented by jealousy — the fear that Rosemary had turned to this good-looking English cousin. And what did this fierce jealousy mean but that he loved her ... loved every hair of her beautiful head. But he was not going to let her know that. Mixed with his love was the still unsatisfied wish to punish her for the trick she had played upon him.

'Well, let Harry go,' he said. 'I don't blame him for trying to help you. I daresay you told him a sad story, and he was always soft-hearted. Now, get your things, my dear. We'll drive home, I've had nothing to eat, and I am hungry and tired. There's a decent hotel a mile or so away. Let's carry on there for food. I hate this squalid Fonda.'

'Paul,' began Rosemary, 'can't you let me go on to Granada — go home without me?'

'No,' he said. 'Your home is at the Villa Lucia.'

'I want to go back to London — to my work — my friend — anything rather than stay with you in Malaga.'

He gave her a queer, cold smile. 'You should not have taken Mercedes' place if you felt so strongly about it.'

She saw that it was like buffeting her

head against a stone wall. Sudden curiosity made her ask: 'How did you trace me here?'

'Little fool,' he said with a low laugh. 'I suppose you thought I was asleep when you left me? I was wide awake, my dear. I waited to see what you would do. I waited until I heard Harry's car go off, then I dressed, got out the Hispano, and followed. A few miles away from Molinos I had a puncture, and lost trace of you. Otherwise I would have been here sooner. But when the tyre was mended it took me an hour to discover which way the car had gone. Finally some peasants directed me up here. And here I am!'

'I see,' said Rosemary hopelessly.

A few minutes later she was seated in her husband's car, beside him, and they were rolling down the white winding road. Maria and her husband had been given forty pesetas by the other señor to hold their peace, and they held it. They had nothing to say when Paul questioned them.

During the next four or five hours Paul and Rosemary had very little to say. They stopped at an hotel for food, then continued the return journey from Molinos to the *hacienda* in the mountains behind Malaga. Rosemary felt like a prisoner who has escaped and been recaptured when they finally drove through the gateway into the lovely gardens of Villa Lucia. Once indoors she collapsed, worn out with the heat, the excitement, the nervous energy wasted this day. As she walked into the cool frescoed hall the world seemed to spin about her. She crumpled at Paul's feet.

He lifted her, and carried her to her room, laid her on the big golden bed which she had deserted at dawn. It was now sunset.

He looked at her for a moment with a queer pang at his heart. She was so white, so piteous, with the dark lashes curving on her cheek, her lips open, as though in silent protest against his tyranny. Suddenly he knelt beside her, and put his dark, handsome head upon her breast.

'Oh, soul of my life, my flower,' he whispered in Spanish. 'My adored wife, why must we go on fighting . . . hurting each other and ourselves . . . when we might love each other so desperately!'

Rosemary recovered consciousness and opened her eyes. When she saw Paul, and the familiar bedroom, a little convulsion shivered through her slender body. She put out both hands, blindly, pushed him away.

'Don't come near me — go away,' she stammered wildly.

Resentment flared up in the man again. He stood up and smiled, tenderness no longer in his eyes.

'Have a good sleep, Rose-Marie, and, when you wake up, just remember that this is your home, 'till death do us part.''

She heard the curt, arrogant voice of the man, and watched him walk, in his imperious way, from her room. She ceased protesting. Passive and mute she lay there with the tears pouring down her cheeks.

From that time onward Rosemary made no further effort to escape from Villa Lucia. She knew that she was watched from all sides. Paul's passionate tyranny was limitless. The more she fought him the harder she made things for herself. His pride, his obstinacy, matched hers. She alternated between hating and admiring him. For what woman in the depths of her heart does not admire the man who is her conqueror?

But her spirit was not yet broken, and nothing would have induced Rosemary to let Paul know that she was resigned. To him she showed always resentment and contempt. And she knew that she could hurt him most deeply by her cold, indifferent acceptance of his embraces. Her lack of response maddened him nowadays. He would kiss her wildly, then fling her from him, and say:

'It is like kissing a statue, *Madre de Dios* . . . I shall find some other woman.'

Rosemary would tell him scornfully, to go, that it did not matter to her at all what he did or how many women he found.

But Don Pablo did not find other women, did not want any woman but his wife.

For a whole month Rosemary stayed there with him at the villa, at his beck and call, performing her duties as mistress of the house, entertaining his friends who called. Before strangers she and Paul were charming to each other. But when they were alone antagonism flamed between them. And when his arms held her they were both of them hostile, unhappy. But neither would give in the fraction of an inch.

During that month Paul heard from his cousin Harry. He showed the letter to Rosemary, and she smiled wryly at the hypocrisy of one paragraph:

'How is your beautiful wife, old man,' he said. 'I hope you're happy, but I'm afraid you can't be under the circumstances. But the girl is to blame — not you. I hope to see you again in Villa Lucia, soon . . . '

Rosemary had no comment to make. Neither did she condescend to show Paul the last letter received from Ida Bryant:

'I am thankful to know you are really well and happy with this barbarian you've married, my dear, but I deplore it. I would so like to be able to see something of you . . . '

Poor old Ida! As Rosemary had anticipated, her friend had been at first dumbfounded and horrified to hear of her marriage only a few weeks after her arrival in Spain. Then, having received one or two long, descriptive letters in which Rosemary told Ida only the satisfactory side of that amazing marriage, Ida grew resigned. Rosemary had deliberately refrained from telling the truth. What good could it do? Ida would only be bewildered and disturbed, and after all, Rosemary had to blame herself, at least, that she was in such a position. It had been Paul's fault in a sense, but equally it was hers for having taken the place of Mercedes Lamanda. Better to allow Ida to believe she was quite content, and it was, after all, the truth, when she said that her husband was rich and powerful and had marvellous properties, and that she was leading a most luxurious life in ideal surroundings.

Eventually she hoped to get poor old Ida out here for a holiday. It would be a fine thing to be able to do something for her, since Paul had so much money to waste. But not until the position was less strained. The last thing Rosemary wished was for Ida to come here with her eagle eye and discover that 'her lamb' was very unhappy, and that the marriage was far from being a success.

One night towards the end of the summer, when the lovely gardens of Villa Lucia were growing brown and baked by the over-fierce sunlight of late summer, Paul gave a dance.

'I wish you to take your proper place as my wife,' he told Rosemary. 'I wish you to entertain the guests I shall choose. You can come with me to Madrid for a day to choose your dress.'

Rosemary accepted this invitation indifferently.

'If it amuses you,' she said.

He flushed hotly. If it amused him? How little it amused him. He wanted nothing but to make Rosemary pay for what she had done to him — surrender everything, body and soul, all her dignity, her pride. And instead he felt that *she was making him* pay, that it was he who accepted defeat.

The dance was held. The flower of southern Spain came to Villa Lucia. The rich and powerful Don Pablo had many friends — members of the

Government, and all anxious to see the beautiful English girl whom he had married, under such amazing circumstances, instead of Mercedes Lamanda.

She was a 'golden girl'. Paul had never seen his wife look more bewitching. The new dress from Madrid was of cloth of gold, fine, glittering, clinging to the exquisite lines of her slim figure. She wore the Iballo diamonds twisted about her slender throat, and a great spray of orchids on her shoulders; a diamond and emerald star on her breast — diamonds on her wrists. Even a tiara of diamonds on her fair head. She hardly recognised herself when Carmenita had finished dressing her. She was no longer the old, simple Rosemary. This was indeed Rose-Marie, a regal young figure, proud, cool, showing nothing of the nervous strain which the pomp and pageant of the reception imposed upon her — save perhaps by the slight trembling of the small gloved hands, clasping a huge ostrich-feather fan.

Paul, in his white uniform and all his military orders on his breast, was himself a magnificent figure, as usual, half a head taller than any other man in the room.

Villa Lucia blazed with lights, was full of flowers. An orchestra played in the reception hall. In the gardens, lanterns burned rosily from every tree. And it was one of those warm, heavy voluptuous nights of the Spanish autumn before the rain and the winds set in. A languorous night, made for love and for lovers.

Don Pablo danced with every woman except his wife, and she danced with every man but her husband. Now and then his dark, moody eyes met her defiant ones. The old antagonism sparked between them electrically. And if he suffered agonies of jealousy when he saw her laughing or smiling at some gay Spaniard, she, perhaps, endured similar pangs that night, while she watched him smile down into the eyes of a pretty woman.

The dance was nearing its end. It had been a huge success. But Rosemary felt suddenly stifled and unutterably lonely in the midst of the glittering crowd. This was her luxurious home, and she was Doña Rosemary Iballo, fêted, flattered, admired. It was all so empty. The taste of ashes was in her mouth. She had been happier, God knew, when she was just Rosemary Wallace in London, going to a cheap cinema with poor old Ida Bryant.

She wandered into the garden, alone, and stood beside a pond full of great waxen lilies. She watched the moonlight drip upon it. Just behind her, a lantern swung from the trees, casting an orange glow on her fair, curling hair, and on her gleaming jewelled young figure.

Paul, watching from the veranda, saw her there. He, too, was weary of the crowd, bored, lonely, miserable. He was sick of conquest by force, of unrequited passion. He wanted the Rose-Marie of the train, with her shy, sweet surrender.

An uncontrollable impulse led him

toward her beautiful golden figure. Then suddenly, in a flash, there was catastrophe. A slight breeze caught the ends of the stiff tulle which she had twisted about her throat before she came into the garden. It drifted up to the lantern close to her head. In a second the filmy material was alight. It looked to the horrified Paul as though fire circled her throat.

He heard her cry of fear, and raced to her.

'*Dios!* Rose-Marie!'

In a moment he had her in his arms, tore the burning tulle from her with his fingers and stamped out the flame. He crushed her against him in an agony of anxiety.

'Rose-Marie, sweet. *Queridissima mia.* Darling — are you hurt?' He spoke in English and Spanish mixed.

She looked up at him, a trifle dazed, and laughed.

'No, I'm not hurt. It only scorched my neck a little. It was so sudden . . . just a shock . . . I'm all right . . . '

'I thought you were all on fire . . . my God . . . what would I have done.'

She looked up at him speechlessly.

This was the old Paul, the tender, boyish, adoring Paul of the train. The blood seemed to rush to her head.

'*Queridissima mia,*' he repeated, and kissed her on the mouth.

For the first time for long weeks, she kissed him back. By a great mutual impulse their lips seemed to merge into that long, impassioned kiss, and their arms clasped each other. They were lost, intoxicated. They were *one*.

For one unbelievable moment it seemed to Rosemary that she had recaptured the lost magic. And then a low familiar voice cut across the silence, close to them.

'Pablo,' it said. 'Oh, Pablo . . . oh, Rose-Marie! . . . '

Paul's arms fell away from his wife. They looked round, and saw a girl standing close to them; a girl in a black dress, with a black shawl about a golden head, and a white, desperate young face. Simultaneously they cried her name:

'Mercedes!'

The girl who had been Mercedes Lamanda put out both hands. Bursting into tears she ran to Paul, and knelt at his feet, and clung on to his arm.

'Oh, Pablo, help me,' she said, in her native tongue. 'Manuel is dead. He died of fever two weeks ago. I am alone and starving. My people have refused me the door. I have no one to come to but you . . . you, Pablo, who once were my promised husband. You won't refuse me help, will you?'

Silence. Rosemary stood motionless. A queer cold feeling crept over her. Paul said in a low, embarrassed voice:

'Of course I will help you, poor little Mercedes.'

Another silence. Rosemary looked at the girl to whom she had been companion. Then a queer, ugly look shot into the brown eyes of the Spanish girl. She pointed a finger at Rosemary:

'You took my place,' she said

hysterically. 'You persuaded me to run away with Manuel. You ruined my life. What are *you* doing here in this *hacienda*, anyway?'

Rosemary drew back, instinctively, from the accusing finger.

'But, Mercedes!' she said in Spanish, her cheeks hot. 'You asked for my help. You ran away because you — why you adored this man, Cadozza.'

'I was a foolish infatuated young girl,' said Mercedes in a sullen voice. 'I didn't realise that he was a stupid temperamental musician who would let me down. We nearly starved. He was thrown out of work. I wished myself back with my parents. Then he caught a chill and died, and it is as well,' she added, with a callousness that astounded Rosemary, who scarcely recognised in this bitter young woman the romantic Spanish girl who had eloped with her lover.

Mercedes turned again to Paul. Her large dark eyes suddenly filled with tears.

'Pablo, *querido mia*, believe me, I was deeply fond of you, but this English companion' — she nodded toward Rosemary — 'constantly talked against you, influenced me against you, and persuaded me to let her take my place as your bride.'

'Oh, Mercedes, that is grossly unfair, and not true!' exclaimed Rosemary hotly. 'Paul' — she appealed to her husband — 'do you believe that?'

He hesitated. Frowning deeply, he looked from one girl to the other. There was, naturally, the shadow of suspicion in his mind that Mercedes spoke the truth. After all, Rosemary *had* obviously influenced Mercedes, and she had done a daring, impudent thing by marrying him in Mercedes' place. Perhaps the poor child, Mercedes, was not altogether to blame. Her face was pale and pathetic and she looked thin and even hungry. His heart began to soften toward her. The fierce passion which had vibrated through his very being for his wife, only a few moments ago, and had seemed to stir and touch her into response . . . was gone.

Rosemary realised that. A chilled feeling replaced her ardour. She, too, had been vibrating with passion . . . had wanted to yield in Paul's arms. But now he suspected her of being the cause of all the trouble. Yes, she could see that. He was inclined to believe Mercedes. Her spirit rose in revolt.

'It's monstrous that you should think I influenced Mercedes against you!' she broke out. 'Paul, I swear, I said and did nothing until she, herself, confessed that she hated you and loved Señor Cadozza.'

'That doesn't seem to matter much now,' said Paul. 'The harm is done.'

Mercedes glanced at Rosemary's hand, noted the wedding-ring, stared at her blazing jewels, her glittering, golden frock. A feeling of rage possessed her.

'Why are you still here?' she demanded. 'You told me the ceremony would be illegal, and that you would return to England.'

'Unfortunately Don Pablo preferred to keep me here. He married me, that day, *knowing* that I was Miss Wallace,' said Rosemary.

She was astonished to discover that she was jealous — yes, actually jealous of this Spanish girl who had once been betrothed to Paul; and angry that she had returned. She was bitterly resentful that the idyll had been interrupted, the beautiful spell broken. Why — why had Mercedes come? Why had that kiss which Paul had laid upon her lips ever ended.

Paul's dark eyes were fixed upon her with that old, hostile, suspicious look, touched with mockery, which she knew so well. He twisted his lips. (How well she knew that cynical, even cruel twist. Oh, Paul, and a moment ago he had kissed her as though he truly loved her!)

'Rose-Marie,' he said. 'You are correct. I did marry you of my own free will, and I did keep you here. But I don't think I ever quite realised that you coerced this young girl into an

171

elopement with Cadozza, just in order that you might hoodwink *me* into marrying *you*.'

Rosemary gasped. She went scarlet, then pale as death. Love and passion were buried in an avalanche of indignation.

'You know that isn't true, Paul. You *know* I never wished to stay here. I've begged and begged you to let me go.'

'Quite. But perhaps you wanted money. You probably counted on that.'

It was the finishing straw. Rosemary turned, speechlessly, and began to walk away. Her eyes stung with tears she was too proud to show.

Mercedes called after her:

'*Si, si!* You did the whole thing to suit yourself. You were a treacherous friend.'

Rosemary swung round.

'Aren't you the traitor, Mercedes?' she said. 'I'd never have believed you would tell such lies, or that *you*, Paul' — she looked at her husband — 'would support such an infamous theory.'

He frowned. A flash of doubt showed

in his fine eyes. Then he remembered her coldness of the last few weeks, her difficult treatment of him, his own defeat at her hands. The thing bit deeply. Don Pablo was spoiled. He shrugged his shoulders.

'Whatever the truth may be, Mercedes has come to me for help, and she shall have it,' he said. 'After all, I treated her badly. I was too indifferent — too careless. I can't blame her for dreading her marriage with me.'

'But I am sorry now, Paul,' Mercedes put in eagerly. 'Ah, *Dio*' — her voice broke — 'I've suffered so, regretted it all. I've been half mad with remorse. I realise now how much I really did care for you, Pablo.'

He turned from her in some embarrassment. But, man-like, he was flattered and touched by the tears that shone in a pair of very beautiful brown eyes, fringed by thick, curling lashes. True eyes of Spain — full of fire, of passion. He was sore with his wife. So long those hazel eyes of hers had regarded him coldly and with hostility. It all came back to him now, and influenced him against Rosemary. He forgot how soft and yielding she had been in his embrace out here in the starlit garden just before Mercedes appeared.

'Poor little Mercedes,' he murmured, and held out a hand to her.

She ran to him, caught his hand, carried it to her lips.

'*Pablo mio* . . . forgive me . . . tell me that you will be my friend.'

'Of course,' he said, moved to tenderness. He patted her head, from which the shawl had fallen, showing the magnificent golden curls.

Mercedes, her head bowed, was inwardly triumphing. Her lips curled at the thought of Rosemary. She hated the English girl, loathed her. She envied her position here as the Doña Rosemary Iballo, her jewels, her triumph. She, Mercedes, meant to win back all those things. Her infatuation for the wretched Manuel had died with his death, and she had had enough of poverty, of disgrace for love's sake!

Rosemary saw the kiss on her husband's hand, and watched him caress Mercedes' head. She walked away with the memory of it wrecking her happiness. Just now, if Mercedes had not come, the gulf between herself and her husband might have been bridged. They might have been united — unutterably happy — that ecstasy of the train recaptured and a marvellous future before them. But Mercedes had spoiled it all.

Rosemary's blood was up. Her mettle was roused. She loved Paul — yes, in her heart of heart she knew that she loved him — madly and passionately. She would not give him back to Mercedes and would not be hounded out of Villa Lucia by them both, no matter what she had done.

She went back to her guests. The dance was continuing. Deliberately Rosemary went on dancing with the man who asked her. She was the most brilliant, lovely, figure of all. But she felt sick at heart because Paul was giving Mercedes shelter.

When the dance ended, and the guests were gone, Don Pablo and his young wife faced each other alone in the deserted reception-room. There were tired lines about Paul's lips and handsome eyes. Rosemary's golden shimmering gown was crushed. The orchids on her shoulder were dead. The close, passionate embrace out in the garden, after the incident of the burnt scarf, had ruined them. She was as white as milk, but her fair young head was flung proudly back, and her hazel eyes defied him.

He looked at her, conscious as usual of the wild thrill of her beauty — a thrill he could never quite control. But to-night he did not intend to be influenced by her charm. He held her responsible for the downfall of Mercedes.

'Understand,' he said. 'Mercedes is to be given every hospitality here as my guest. I have handed her over to Maria and Carmenita, and she is sleeping in the Flower Room, now.'

Rosemary clenched her hands. The Flower Room was the loveliest guest-room in Villa Lucia, preserved for the most honoured friends.

'You have soon forgiven your former fiancée for deserting you,' she said.

'It is easy to forgive a poor child who was merely infatuated by this Cadozza, and who was influenced by a scheming woman.'

'Don't dare to repeat that lie, Paul; and remember I am only a very few years older than Mercedes.'

He bowed, a cold smile curling his lips.

'Very well. Good night, Doña Rose-Marie Iballo.'

Rosemary swallowed hard.

'I would leave Villa Lucia at once,' she said, in a choked voice, 'only . . . '

'What?' He lifted an eyebrow.

'This is now my home. So far I have been a prisoner, but now I stay . . . of my own free will. I do not intend to allow Mercedes to take my place.'

That put a new complexion on the matter. Paul was mildly amused. But he could not believe that Rosemary wished to stay on his account. For too long she had lain passive in his arms, refusing him her kisses. Now, it was obvious, she wanted his money . . . and perhaps she had other, ulterior, motives for remaining. He laughed.

'Are you jealous, my dear? Because I must confess Mercedes has become interesting since her elopement and widowhood . . . quite alluring, in fact. Do you mind?'

Rosemary shook from head to foot.

'You cad!' she said.

She turned and walked from the room.

And that was the end to the night of stars, of music, of beauty, which had drawn them together — only to fling them further than ever apart.

5

During the next few days there followed a new kind of contest between Paul and Rosemary. A silent fight — of passionate pride and jealousy. Rosemary wanted this husband of hers now — wanted him — meant to keep him. And, on his side, there was the old passion for her which he could not stifle, and mingled with it, hostility and suspicion, daily fostered by Mercedes.

Mercedes remained at Villa Lucia, an honoured guest. It did not matter so much now that her parents disowned her and shut the gates of the Villa Santa Barbara to her. She had lived in poverty with Manuel Cadozza, since when her passion for him had died. There now burned a far fiercer flame of love for her former fiancé. She was older, more mature, since her elopement and her husband's speedy death. She was a woman — ardent — greedy — anxious to recapture Don Pablo, his wealth and title.

Every day she encountered her former companion. And now she was the guest, and Rosemary the hostess. Never had Rosemary been prouder, more dignified, more actively mistress of the Villa. She was icily polite to Mercedes, and Mercedes to her. Paul looked on . . . half amused, half annoyed, and wholly dissatisfied with life. He was still a slave to his deep-rooted passion for his wife. But he never entered her room these days, and had barely touched her hand since their big moment on the night of the dance. Half in jest, half out of the wish to punish Rosemary, he made himself especially charming to Mercedes.

So the game went on.

And then, out of the blue, Harry Dyall returned to the scene. But not to Villa Lucia. He came to the Caleta Palace Hotel in Malaga.

Harry Dyall had not finished with Rosemary. She had given him the cold shoulder, and Paul had carried her off again, but Harry was undaunted. He was still determined to make Rosemary go away with him. Even deeper was his ambition to rob his cousin of everything — money, title, estates.

He did not mean to appear boldly at the Villa Lucia. He went to work with more cunning. He was going from bad to worse, and he was drinking heavily. At moments, when his brain was inflamed by drink, he conjured up all kinds of mad visions of Rosemary as *his* wife, of himself living in Paul's beautiful *hacienda*, and of Paul lying dead. Then there would be no fear that he would be disinherited, or of Rosemary giving Paul a son and heir.

One September evening, slightly intoxicated, Harry drove from Malaga up the mountain, stopped the car a few yards from Villa Lucia, and then strolled as far as the beautiful wrought-iron gateway of his cousin's home. He

181

looked moodily up the drive of palms. He thought:

'Paul has everything, damn him! Why can't I take his place?'

A slim girl, with fair hair half veiled by a black lace mantilla, came round a curve in the road, and started to walk past him. He thought it was the woman of his desire.

'Rosemary!' he said eagerly.

She turned, and Harry Dyall saw that it was not Rosemary, but a girl with pale, cameo-like face, and great burning black eyes. Only the daffodil-coloured hair was like Rosemary's.

Harry made an apology in Spanish. The girl stared at him inquisitively.

'You want — the Doña Rosemary Iballo?'

'I — would like to see her.'

Mercedes drew nearer. She was interested. Who was this tall Englishman with the blue, slightly bloodshot eyes and flushed face? Had Rosemary a lover? That would be exciting, and excellent news for her to pass on to

Paul to incense him further against his wife.

'I am a guest at Villa Lucia,' she said. 'And you?'

'My name is Harry — ' he began, and then paused, wondering whether he did wisely to give himself away to a stranger. He was astonished when she said swiftly:

'Ah — you are Paul's cousin from England — Mr. Dyall!'

'How do you know, señorita?'

'Señora,' she corrected. 'I am widowed. I know, because I am — or was — Mercedes Lamanda, once engaged to your cousin.'

Harry bowed over the hand she extended.

'I am enchanted,' he said. Nobody could be more charming than Harry when he chose. 'And you are a *guest*! Of the lovely Doña Rosemary?'

Mercedes black eyes flashed.

'Scarcely. But of Paul's. My husband is dead. Paul is giving me shelter. Rosemary hates me. It was she who did me out of all this — who persuaded me to abandon Paul just before our marriage.'

Harry raised his brows. He was just sobering up, and very intrigued. He felt that the dark-eyed Spanish girl might be an ally if he worked things well. He bowed again.

'Señora . . . will you go for a little walk with me? There is much I would like to talk about — including the dissolution of the marriage of my excellent cousin and his charming wife. Frankly there is nothing I want more. And you?'

Mercedes' pulse thrilled.

'You wish the marriage done away with?'

'Yes. I happen to be very much in love with Rosemary.'

Harry told that particular story because he hesitated to suggest that it was Paul's money that he wanted.

'Ah!' said Mercedes. 'And I love Paul. Therefore . . . '

'Therefore, señora,' said Harry Dyall

softly, 'let us walk and talk things over.'

They turned, and strolled together through the swift-falling darkness.

After half an hour's conversation, these two understood each other. The separation of Paul and Rosemary was the one desirable thought they shared. Both greedy and mean, the man was inflamed by his unscrupulous ambitions, and the girl by a new and feverish passion for all that she had once abandoned for love's sake.

And by mutual consent, scarcely daring to look at each other, they reached another conclusion. That there must be attempted crime at Villa Lucia, and that Rosemary must be the suspect, the accused.

'Just a harmless white powder,' Harry Dyall whispered to Mercedes. 'It will do nothing but make my cousin very sick, but it is quite safe.'

Mercedes bit hard on red lips that were paling with emotion from such terrible thoughts.

'*Madre di Dios*; but are you sure,

señor? I want Pablo. As I value my life, I value his. The powder will not do him injury?'

Harry Dyall lied shamelessly.

'I swear it. It is harmless — just a little drug given to me by a native when I was out East . . . and no ordinary doctor here could diagnose the illness of a person who has taken it. Rosemary must give it to him. You will pour out the wine which he drinks after dinner, having first put the powder into his glass. You will pretend to be sorry for past quarrels, and to wish to celebrate peace between yourselves. Paul, for a certainty, will drink. When he is ill, later, you will go to him and say you suspect Rosemary of villainy. Then a little packet will be found — say in her jewel-case? Paul will never believe in her again. He will send her away. I will take care that she never returns to Spain, and of course he will find the consolation he needs in *your* arms, señora. Is it not so?'

Mercedes listened to all this, her

breath bated, her cheeks pale. There was moisture on the palms of her hands. She was fascinated, yet repelled, by the idea. She wanted to get Rosemary away, yet feared to hurt Paul.

'You are positive!' she said. 'The powder cannot hurt Pablo?'

'I swear it.'

'Then give it to me,' said Mercedes. She looked down the avenue of palms toward the white *hacienda*, her whole body shaking.

Harry bowed, and mopped his wet forehead with a handkerchief. He felt hot, almost stifled. He knew that he was contemplating something akin to murder when he arranged that Mercedes should meet him outside the gates in half an hour's time to receive the drug which he would bring her from his hotel in Malaga.

And he was half afraid.

That night a rainstorm broke over the mountains, and a cold wind shook the palm-trees in the gardens of Villa Lucia.

Rosemary ordered the servants to light a great log-fire in the beautiful library. She was feeling deeply depressed to-night, although she preserved a brave, proud exterior. Not by word or sign did she betray to Paul or Mercedes what she was suffering. There was an incessant ache in her heart now, when Paul was present — an ache of longing to reach again that pinnacle of ecstasy which they had shared in the garden before Mercedes came. She was bitterly resentful of Mercedes' presence — of the fact that she was a constant third in the home. She, Paul's wife, was never alone with him. And beyond being icily polite before the servants, or taunting her when Mercedes was there, he did not speak to her. He seemed to have made up his mind that she was an adventuress who had helped to ruin Mercedes and deliberately entrapped him. He had lost sight of all her good points, of all his former faith in her. Only her beauty and grace fired him when he was close to her. Nowadays, even his passion he controlled.

Rosemary tried to make up her mind to appeal to Paul to believe in her again. Surely he must believe it, she told herself. He must remember her unhappiness when he had kept her a prisoner. That did not look as though she had meant to stay. Surely he would meet her half way if just once she stifled pride and told him that she loved him much more now than in the train, in the first flush of their passion.

On this stormy evening she chose her loveliest frock. Black velvet, sweeping to little red shoes with long Tudor sleeves of the same lacquer red. Mercedes was in black, the young widow, complete, simulating remorse for the past. A very pretty pose, while inwardly she raged like a young tigress to take the Doña Rosemary Iballo's place.

During dinner Rosemary made one attempt to be gay and friendly. Paul was bitter, satirical in response. But Mercedes, seizing this chance, met Rosemary half way, and held out an olive-branch. When dinner was over, she herself stayed behind in the dining-hall, after the others had gone, and poured out three glasses of wine, which she placed on a silver salver. Into the left-hand one she emptied the powder which Harry Dyall had given her. She did so with a feeling of distaste. But she did not falter. The blood of Spanish Inquisitors ran in the veins of Mercedes Lamanda.

She carried the salver into the *salon*. Paul was smoking a cigarette, staring out of one of the long windows. Rosemary, lovely, charming enough in her black and red dress, stood just behind him, her lips wistful, her eyes appealing.

'Paul. I want to tell you something — ' she began almost shyly.

Mercedes interrupted that speech very quickly.

'Rose-Marie — Pablo!' she said gaily. 'I have decided that we three have been enemies long enough. Why not let us be friends? Why not drink to future happiness — to a working out of this unhappy problem.'

Rosemary, quite deceived, was touched by this.

'You are right, Mercedes. It's so silly to behave as though we were all enemies, isn't it, Paul?'

Paul shrugged his shoulders, and made a short, bitter retort, but he seemed indifferent, and held out his hand for a glass.

'I'll drink to anything, but I'll believe in nothing,' he said.

'Give him the left-hand glass,' whispered Mercedes to Rosemary. 'It has the most in it.'

Rosemary lifted the glass, and walked with it to Paul. She was utterly unsuspicious of foul play, and in the mood to appeal to her handsome husband. She gave the wine to him with a swift, pretty gesture and said: 'See, *Pablo mio*, I've chosen the biggest glass for you. Now drink, and let us forget the past and smile again.'

His heart jerked as he looked down at

her. Heavens! To see her in this mood — beseeching — enchanting — so different to the cold, passive wife who had maddened him with her indifference. How could it fail to disturb him — to make him suddenly forget everything, Mercedes included?

He went very pale with repressed emotion, and seized the glass from her. Mercedes watched, breathless. Rosemary could have said nothing more incriminating. *She* had chosen that fatal glass for him . . .

Don Pablo lifted the wine to his lips, and drained it to the dregs.

★　★　★

Mercedes watched Paul drain that glass. Her face was livid. Her eyes grew wide with sudden terror. What had she done? Was Harry Dyall to be trusted? *Was that powder harmless? Madre de Dios*; what if Paul died and she was the instrument of his death! Nobody would know, Rosemary would be blamed. But she, Mercedes, would have it on her immortal soul.

She turned away to hide her agitation, and began to interest herself in a book. Rosemary, unconscious of villainy, watched her husband with shining eyes. The look he had given her just now was of renewed tenderness and passion. That wonderful, thrilling look which had magnetised her on the night in the Madrid express. The look that seemed to tear her very heart from her body and dissolve it into his being. With tremendous stirring of all that was most womanly and passionate in her, Rosemary drank her own wine, then set down the glass and smiled at Paul.

'Is it peace between thee and me?' she whispered, in his own language.

He put his glass on the table, and wiped his lips with a silk handkerchief. His brilliant eyes searched every feature of his wife's face. She was so beautiful. She smiled at him so exquisitely. What could it mean but that Rosemary really cared for him? She wanted peace between them.

Perhaps she was not what Mercedes had tried to make him believe. Neither mercenary nor unprincipled. Perhaps there had been grave misunderstandings, unfounded doubts.

Don Pablo was fired with the sudden longing to end the enmity and misunderstanding between himself and his wife. He forgot Mercedes. He forgot the other side of him which had wanted to hurt, to break, his wife. He came close to her, and, although he did not touch her, he gave her an expressive look, more eloquent than physical contact.

'*Alma de mia vida*,' he whispered. 'Did you truly wish to give me that wine so that I could drink a toast to peace between us? Do you love me, Rose-Marie?'

The rich blood sprang to Rosemary's face and throat. She trembled. She was no longer conscious of Mercedes' presence in the room, but only of Paul, who no longer looked at her with cruelty or bitterness. Pressing her hands to her breast, she whispered:

'Paul . . . *Pablo mio!*'

He grew dazed with the sheer allure of her. She was wonderful, in her clinging velvet dress, and with the light shining upon her fair blonde head. He took one of her hands and crushed it in his.

'Rose-Marie,' he said. 'Come with me to the library. There's a book there . . . I want to show you . . . '

She knew it was no book he wanted. It was her arms, her lips, he desired. Every fibre of her leapt in warm response. She gave a little broken laugh and let him lead her from the room.

Mercedes closed her book with a snap. She looked ghastly.

'*Dios — Dios,*' she said through her teeth. 'If this Englishman has fooled me . . . '

She was like a fiend with bitter jealousy of Rosemary. She had seen Paul's face — watched him grow drunk with longing for Rosemary. And they had gone to the library to find a book. Well, she knew better than that. It was to effect a reconciliation. All her work of the last few weeks was to be undone . . . wasted.

What of this dope that would make Paul temporarily ill? How long did it take to work? What if Harry Dyall had made an error?

Mercedes walked out of the drawing-room and ran upstairs. She made certain that Carmenita, Rosemary's maid, was down at her supper, and that there was nobody about. She stole into Rosemary's beautiful bedroom and shut the door behind her.

Moving noiselessly, like a cat, Mercedes rummaged round until she discovered a drawer in the dressing-table which held Rosemary's jewel-case. The case was unlocked. Rosemary had taken out one of the valuable Iballo rings to wear to-night, and had not locked the case up again.

Mercedes drew a small white packet from her pocket, and a crumpled paper containing a speck of powder, both of which she placed in the under-tray of the jewel-case. Then she shut it again.

'Now, Rose-Marie,' she thought venomously, 'if there is trouble — it will be *you* who have done this thing. If crime it is, *you* shall be the criminal!'

She stole out of the bedroom and downstairs again, and then paused outside the library and listened a second to lowered voices.

In that room Rosemary was tasting the sweets of Paradise, only to have them dashed from her lips in a very brief while. When they were alone in the dim, beautiful room, with its priceless books and great log-fire leaping in the open grate, Paul told her at once what lay in his heart.

'Rose-Marie, darling,' he said in English. 'Have I been wrong? Do you care a little whether there is peace between us or not?'

She swallowed hard.

'Paul, I've always cared. But you made things so hard. It wasn't your money I wanted. Mercedes has lied and misled you. I'm not like that, Paul, I'd willingly give up all the luxury and wonder of Villa Lucia to go with you to a humble cottage in the mountains . . . where you would love me and believe in me.'

The man's heart leapt. There was a queer, burning sensation in his throat, and a blinding pain in his head, which worried him. But he tried not to notice this. For the moment passion, ecstasy, were dominant. He held out his arms.

'Sweet — my beautiful — is it really true? Do you care for me? You're not what Mercedes thinks . . . what she wants me to think?'

'No, Paul. I am just the Rose-Marie of the train, who tore her heart from her breast and gave it to you.'

All cruelty and cynicism were wiped from Don Pablo's face. He looked strangely young and handsome.

'Sweet,' he said again. 'Then it *shall* be peace between us, and more than peace . . . '

He went swiftly down on one knee at her feet and kissed her ankles.

She looked down at the bent, dark head, and adored him. She knew beyond all doubt that she loved this man whom she had married under such strange circumstances. More than loved — she worshipped him. Pride was buried; past grievances forgotten. All that she had suffered at his hands was wiped out.

'Oh, Paul . . . darling, darling Paul,' she said, her eyes full of tears. 'Oh, my dearest! . . . '

He stood up and swept her into a close, fierce embrace. The pain in his head was growing worse. He felt strangely sick and ill. All his limbs were becoming leaden, and a cold sweat broke out over him. He failed to understand it. For an instant he held Rosemary close, and kissed her cool, marble shoulder, and her soft throat.

She locked her arms about his neck, leaned back, her eyes shut. In this embrace she felt as though her very spirit and his were merging into one.

Then she felt him shivering, and saw to her horror that his cheeks were greyish and his forehead dripping wet. She drew away from him.

'Paul, darling . . . Paul . . . what is it?'

He moistened his lips with his tongue, and put a hand to his throat.

'*Madonna* . . . I'm ill,' he muttered in Spanish. 'Something is hurting me . . . *Madre de Dios* . . . it burns . . . I'm ill!'

He no longer held her. It was she who supported him in her strong young arms. He was swaying on his feet.

'My God, what's wrong? What's happened to you, Paul.'

His eyes became suffused, and an expression of acute agony convulsed his features.

'I'm ill . . . poisoned . . . yes, I am poisoned,' he panted. '*Santa Maria* . . . '

The last word was a groan of agony. He could no longer stand. He was too heavy for Rosemary and he slithered through her arms on to the floor, and lay there, writhing.

She looked down at him in horror. Paul saying that he was *poisoned* . . . . God in heaven, what was happening now? She screamed:

'Mercedes! Pietro! . . . Carmenita! . . . '

She went down on her knees, and lifted Paul's head on to her lap. He was a leaden colour, and in agony. He could not speak, but his eyes beseeched her to put him out of his pain. It was unbearable when she loved him so, and she was horribly frightened.

'Darling Paul . . . oh, my darling . . . what is it?'

With a little lace handkerchief she wiped his lips.

The library door opened, and Mercedes and one or two servants rushed in.

Rosemary looked up.

'Don Pablo has been taken ill. Pietro, telephone for the doctor,' she panted, addressing Paul's valet. Then to her maid: 'Carmenita, prepare the bed . . . hot-water bottles . . . blankets . . . at once.'

'*Si, si.*' Carmenita glanced at her master, and crossed herself with superstitious horror. Certainly he looked as though a devil possessed him, with his knees drawn up and his face contracted in mortal pain.

Like frightened sheep the servants scattered to do Rosemary's bidding. Mercedes remained, looking down at Paul. She had a hand to her lips, and her eyes were wide and afraid. But she was calm.

'I can't think what has happened,' panted Rosemary. 'He thinks he has been poisoned. But I don't see why? He has eaten nothing that we have not had. The fish for dinner was good, wasn't it? Oh, he is in awful pain. Isn't it horrible?'

'Yes, it is horrible,' agreed Mercedes in a strange voice. 'And obviously he has been poisoned. *Si, si,* and *by whom?*'

Rosemary stood up and faced the Spanish girl.

'You're not suggesting that he has

been deliberately poisoned by somebody?'

'What else can have happened?'

'That is ridiculous. Who bears him a grudge?'

Mercedes looked at her slyly under her long heavy lashes.

'Perhaps you?'

'Are you mad?'

'No. But I alone saw what you did. You gave Pablo the wine. What was in that glass that you chose for him?'

Rosemary stared, then gave a quick nervous laugh.

'You *are* insane to suggest such a thing.'

'Not at all. Just now, when you left me, I picked up his glass. There are dregs in it. They smelt queer. I wondered what it was. You gave it to him, didn't you?'

Rosemary's face was frozen with horror now.

'Good God, what an infamous suggestion!'

'But it is true.'

Mercedes burst into tears, and flung herself down on the floor beside Paul.

'*Pablo mio*, she has poisoned you, this wicked girl . . . she has tried to murder you. Pablo . . . Pablo!'

There was an instant of stupefied silence. Rosemary was so horrified by the unexpected accusation that she felt unable to move or speak. Then Paul stirred and opened his eyes. Immediately Rosemary knelt down and put a cushion under his head.

'Are you better, darling?'

'Don't listen to her, Pablo; she has tried to poison you!' Mercedes wept hysterically. 'I know it . . . I know it . . . don't listen to her.'

Paul's heavy eyes looked up into Rosemary's. They were no longer brilliant with passionate love for her. They were tortured and suspicious.

'What have . . . you . . . done . . . ?' he said with difficulty. 'You gave me . . . that wine . . . it was poisoned . . . *you*.'

Rosemary could not even answer. Her tongue clove to the roof of her mouth. Mutely she stared at him. He did not speak again. His eyelids drooped, and he fell back unconscious. The door opened. A doctor and a crowd of servants rushed in. Mercedes continued to wail:

'Don Pablo has been poisoned . . . poisoned by his wife . . . '

The servants made a ring around them, the women weeping, repeatedly crossing themselves, the men muttering. They all loved their master, and they were horrified by his ghastly appearance. The doctor, a short Spaniard with a pointed beard and glasses, carrying a little black bag, knelt down beside Paul, and began to unbutton his waistcoat.

'What have we here?' he muttered in his own language.

'He has been poisoned!' began Mercedes.

Then Rosemary took command. Never before in her life had she felt more mistress of herself. She turned blazing eyes upon the Spanish girl.

'Leave this room, and stop scream-ing,' she said sternly. 'You have done enough harm already.'

To the servants she gave a sharp order.

'Go. I will ring if you are needed. Pietro, you and Andres stay behind to carry your master to his bedroom.'

Mercedes saw that this was no time to argue with Rosemary. She had done harm enough, Rosemary said. Perhaps that was true. With a handkerchief pressed to her eyes she moved out of the library, and the other servants followed, chattering and gesticulating. They had all heard what the señora had said. *Dios!* But it was terrible if the English *espousa* of Don Pablo, had, in truth, attempted to poison him.

The servants-hall of the *hacienda* buzzed with rumour and morbid curiosity.

Rosemary, in the library, looked down at the doctor, who was making an examination of Paul.

She pressed her ice-cold hands

together. She felt that she could scarcely breathe. She had been through a great many disasters since she came to Spain. But this was the worst of all. She felt that she must wake at any moment to find that she was passing through an incredible nightmare. Or lift her eyes and find that she was looking upon a lurid drama of the screen . . . and that Ida was beside her, sucking peppermints, laughing at the depicted agonies of the figures which flashed before their eyes.

It could not be true that she, Rosemary, was this Doña Rosemary, the central figure of a real and grim drama, and that she was being accused of poisoning her own husband.

The doctor looked up. He addressed the beautiful English wife of his most wealthy and illustrious patient with great deference.

'Of a certainty Don Pablo is gravely ill and suffering from the effects of poison. Can the Doña Rosemary tell me what he has eaten to-night?'

Breathing quickly, Rosemary acquainted the *medico* with the evening's menu. Soup, risotto, veal, and a rich cream sweet of which Don Pablo was particularly fond. And with it he had drunk sherry, and then *vino blanco* . . . and, afterwards, coffee. Black and unsweetened, he took it. But they had all had the same, and nobody else was ill. She could not begin to understand it.

The little doctor stood up, stroking his beard.

'*Si, si*; it is extraordinary. And what had the señora meant when she had talked about poison?'

Rosemary, white and stern, flung back her head.

'The señora must be out of her mind. She talks about poison in the wine which Don Pablo drank later in the evening.'

'You shall see the glass,' added Rosemary. 'You shall make your examination of it, and report to me.'

The doctor bowed. With some curiosity he eyed the Doña Rosemary through his strong magnifying glasses. He had attended Don Pablo before . . . and he knew all the Iballos. And of course he had heard of the amazing marriage which had been contracted between Don Pablo and the English girl in Malaga. He could not understand why the Lamanda girl was here. It was rumoured in Malaga that she had eloped to Barcelona with a musician. Why, then, was she in the Iballo *hacienda?* And, *per Dios*, the English girl was a lovely lady. She looked white and frightened, but she was as fair and beautiful as a lily in her graceful velvet gown.

'Do not distress yourself unnecessarily,' he murmured with Spanish gallantry. 'I will do all I can for your husband. Let the men carry him to his room. He must have a strong emetic immediately.'

Rosemary gave the servants their orders.

The unconscious Paul was lifted and taken carefully upstairs to his room. Rosemary followed with the doctor. She

209

felt dazed and spent. If that wine *had* been poisoned, she could guess that Mercedes herself must be responsible. Appalling thought! But that did not matter. Nothing mattered but Paul, and if Paul died to-night Rosemary felt that she herself would not wish to live.

The doctor would not allow her in Paul's room now. He and the valet were attending to the unfortunate Don Pablo. Mercedes had retired to her own room. But Rosemary could not attempt to rest. And it was in this hour that she made up her mind to send for Ida Bryant. She was facing too much alone. She wanted her stern, sensible, practical friend, Ida, with her homely face and motherly affection. She, Rosemary was the wife of a wealthy man. She could well afford to send Ida her fare and keep her here. Paul could not object. She had entertained Mercedes at his bidding. Now he must accept one of her English friends.

For the first time in her life, Rosemary took money that did not actually belong to her. She knew that her husband kept a roll of notes in his desk with which he paid the servants. Well, she would borrow that until Paul was well enough to discuss matters. Deliberately Rosemary put the necessary money in an envelope and rang for one of the menservants. She was going to send an urgent summons to Ida, and wire her the necessary cash. Of course it would mean her losing her job. But Paul must compensate her for that. There were many things that Paul must do when he was better. And of course he *would* get better. Rosemary refused to face any other probability. So the wire to Ida went speeding across the Continent: *'Come at once, I need you. Rosemary.'*

6

There followed the most terrible night in Rosemary's memory.

For hours Don Pablo was violently ill — so ill that the doctor wondered if he would live. Spasm after spasm seized and convulsed him. Now and then, brave though he was, he found it hard to keep the groans of agony from escaping him.

Rosemary heard those groans, and, despite the doctor's reluctance to admit her, insisted upon being at Paul's bedside. She held on to his hand. Barely conscious, he clung to her in his suffering, and she shared his pain, torn with compassion. She felt that she would willingly give her life to spare him.

The little doctor was frankly puzzled. He made his examination of the glass from which Don Pablo had drunk, and could find no trace of ordinary poison in the wine. But the whitish powder, hysterically condemned by Mercedes, was certainly peculiar, and could not be accounted for.

He could not diagnose the case beyond the fact that Don Pablo was suffering from some form of poison.

Mercedes prowled around like a nervous cat. She was not yet satisfied. Harry Dyall's powder had certainly done efficient work, and Pablo suspected his wife. But if he died . . .

Paul, however, did not die. He had a magnificent constitution, and both the doctor and Rosemary worked indefatigably all night long to help him.

When those hellish hours of pain and sickness were passed, and the grey dawn broke over Villa Lucia, Paul was out of danger and much better.

The first pink and amber rays of morning crept through the half-open shutters into the room where he was lying, and found him sleeping naturally.

The doctor went home, tired but

satisfied. Everybody in the *hacienda*, including Mercedes, breathed again. Rosemary, utterly exhausted, knelt by her husband's bed, the tears pouring down her cheeks. He was all right. He was not going to die. She thanked God. But it distressed her immeasurably to see how that terrible night had ravaged him. His cheeks seemed sunken. He was drawn and pale, and there were heavy black rings under his eyes.

She seized one of his brown, sensitive hands, and covered it with kisses.

'My dear, my darling; thank God you are all right.'

He was asleep and could not hear. He did not know that she had watched and worked all night beside him. But as Rosemary tiptoed from the room, and shut the door quietly behind her, Mercedes met her in the passage, and whispered venomously:

'What right have you in that room? You tried to murder him?'

Rosemary, cold and white, looked at the Spanish girl sternly.

'You're out of your mind, Mercedes. The trouble you have passed through recently has really distorted your imagination. You know perfectly well that I am not responsible for what happened last night.'

'Then who is?'

'Perhaps you, Mercedes.'

Mercedes' black lashes drooped. She gave a sneering little laugh.

'Naturally you would try to put the blame on somebody else. I adore Pablo. I wouldn't harm a hair of his head.'

'Neither would I, Mercedes — and well you know it.'

'I doubt that. Paul has doubts too.'

Rosemary suddenly blazed into temper.

'Listen, I have had enough of your insolence!' she said violently in Spanish. 'I am Don Pablo's wife, and I order you to leave my home.'

'Many thanks, but I take my orders only from Don Pablo,' was Mercedes' answer. 'And do not boast of your position, because it will be you who will leave Villa Lucia — and very soon.'

Rosemary walked past her without a word. She walked to her room. She was so tired that she could scarcely stand. Her whole body ached. It had been a terrible, unforgettable, night.

She took off the velvet dress. One sleeve was almost torn from it, and the velvet was crushed and stained. Paul had clutched at her in his spasms of agony. Her heart contracted at the memory of his suffering. It seemed difficult to believe that anybody could make such a brutal attempt on his life. And of course Mercedes Lamanda was responsible. The girl was rotten all through. She would stop at nothing to gain her own end. And the desired end was, of course, the expulsion of her, Rosemary, from Villa Lucia.

Exhausted, Rosemary lay on her bed and tried to sleep awhile. And her last thought was:

'Ida . . . dear old Ida . . . I hope to God you come and help me through this. I can't face them all by myself much longer.'

She slept, through sheer exhaustion, until late in the morning. Her first action was to ring for Carmenita and ask for news of the master. Carmenita assured her that he was better and had slept until an hour ago.

Hastily Rosemary drank the coffee and ate the roll which Carmenita brought her, then took her bath and put on a thin white silk dress. It was going to be another of those languorous days of the Spanish autumn.

With some trepidation Rosemary entered her husband's room. Paul was almost himself again. The effects of the curious Eastern poison were not long lasting. He was sitting up in bed, drinking strong black coffee. But he looked ill, sombre, and bitterly hostile when he regarded his young wife.

Rosemary paused in the middle of the room. Mercedes, who seemed to Rosemary like a bird of ill omen in her black widow's attire, was already there, sitting beside the sick man.

Rosemary was just in time to hear

her say: 'You can't possibly believe in that wicked woman. You will be a dead man if you allow her to remain here.'

Silence. Paul set his coffee cup on the table beside the bed, and lit a cigarette, then almost immediately stubbed it on the tray as though the taste were unpleasant. Rosemary advanced to the foot of the bed. Her cheeks were pink with hot, nervous colour, but her lips were firm.

'Paul; there must be an end to this,' she said in English. 'Mercedes is out of her mind, and I demand that she leaves our house at once.'

'*Uno momento* . . . one moment,' Paul replied in Spanish. 'I'm not going to do anything in a hurry. But I will get to the bottom of this. Last night an attempt was made on my life. Had I drunk a little more of that wine, and the doctor's remedies been less effective, I might now be a corpse. Some mysterious powder was put in my wine. It was *poison*. You, Rose-Marie, gave me that wine, and chose that particular glass for me. Do you remember?'

'Yes, I remember,' she said in a low voice. Cold as ice she looked down at him. She was cut to the quick by his horrible suspicions.

'And Mercedes tells me that you poured out that wine in the dining-room, and left her to carry in the tray.'

Rosemary began to tremble violently.

'That isn't true.'

'Also,' continued Paul, 'she tells me that she chanced to pass your bedroom door this evening. It was half open. She glanced in. You did not realise that you were overlooked. She saw you put a little white packet in your jewel-case. She tells me that she wondered if you were taking drugs, and it worried her. Now, naturally, she thinks that packet may have something to do with what occurred last night.'

Rosemary clenched her hands so tightly that her nails almost pierced the soft palms. Her face was as white as her dress.

'What an infamous suggestion. Good

God, Paul, can't you see that it's all a wicked fabrication? Why should I wish to poison you? Don't you realise yet . . . I love you with all my heart?'

His lips took that cruel and cynical twist which she dreaded.

'A bit difficult for me to credit that, my charming wife. Earlier to-day, Mercedes saw you with my cousin Harry. I hear that he has come back secretly to visit you. I have often wondered when you went away with him whether he attracted you . . . as I did in the train.'

Speechlessly she stared at him. Insults from Paul, and worse from Mercedes. Lie after lie . . . blow after blow.

She broke out: 'Why do you believe all these things that Mercedes tells you? Why should you believe her before me? I didn't even know that your cousin was in Spain again.'

'La! La!' put in Mercedes. 'I myself saw you with him outside the gates.'

'Perhaps both you and my cousin

Harry are trying to get rid of me,' said Don Pablo with a freezing smile. 'It would be an excellent plan. My wife and my heir ... to hasten me to my grave, and then enjoy my money together.'

Rosemary, quivering from head to foot, gave him a look of speechless horror. It seemed impossible that he should say such things ... when so often he had held her in his arms and called her his adored wife.

The tears sprang to her eyes.

'Paul, you are the victim of the most awful villainy ... but it isn't mine. You're still ill ... you must be ... otherwise you couldn't say such ghastly things to me ... couldn't even think of them!'

'Send for her jewel-case ... send for it, then, and let her unlock it before you,' put in Mercedes.

'If that is your feeble story we'll soon disprove it,' said Rosemary.

She rang the bell, and to Pietro, who entered, she said: 'Tell Carmenita to

221

bring my jewel-case here at once.'

Paul lay back on his pillows, frowning, and Mercedes examined the tip of her toe, a little smile playing about her lips.

Rosemary saw that smile, and wondered, in horror, to what lengths this girl would go to satisfy her unscrupulous ambitions.

So Harry was in Spain! Harry had been here, close to Villa Lucia. It explained a lot. She knew for a certainty that he was an unprincipled rogue, and it was time that he was exposed to Paul. If only she could make Paul believe in her . . .

Carmenita appeared with the scarlet leather case which contained the Iballo jewels. Rosemary took it, dismissed her, then handed the case to her husband.

'Look through it,' she said coldly.

Almost reluctantly he obeyed her. He was sick to the very soul about the whole business. And even now, suspecting Rosemary of the worst possible crime, he could not forget her beauty, her sweetness, which had intoxicated him yesterday. But he came of a fierce, suspicious race, easily over-excited and persuaded. Mercedes had put in a good half hour with him before his wife appeared this morning.

He began to look through the jewel-case. Mercedes watched, her heart pounding in her breast. Rosemary looked on indifferently. But very soon her pulse gave a horrid jerk. From beneath a pile of precious stones, Paul lifted a tiny sealed packet, and then an empty crumpled one. The latter he unfolded and raised to his nostrils. Then he looked up at Rosemary, his dark eyes widening with horror.

'*Madre de Dios*, it is the same odour that came from my wine. Mercedes was right. Here is the powder. You, my wife, wish to hasten me to the family vault so that you might enjoy my fortune with a new lover, eh?'

Rosemary gave a gasping cry.

'Paul, this is sheer villainy. It is Mercedes who put those packets in my jewel-case. On my sacred oath I swear that I know nothing about it. Would I have been so ready to let you look through the case if I had known that they were there?'

He looked back at her. There was more than horror in his heart. There was consuming grief. He had loved her to the pitch of madness. It was a staggering blow to discover that she wished to murder him. On the other hand, what she said had its points. She would not so readily have sent for the case if she had known that the powder was there. What, in the name of heaven, did it all mean, and in whom was he to believe?

He put his hands to his swimming head. He was deathly pale and weak.

'I don't know what to think. My brain is reeling,' he said in a hollow voice.

'You must believe me,' said Rosemary.

'*Pablo mio,*' put in Mercedes, rising to her feet. 'I implore you not to listen to this wicked English girl.'

'I wonder *you're* not afraid to do these terrible things,' Rosemary said to her, panting. 'You who practise a religion and make the sign of the Cross upon yourself night and morning.'

Mercedes shrank a little. She passed the tip of her tongue over lips that were dry. She felt none too happy about the situation, but she was so far implicated now that she had to go on, otherwise she would face her own ruin. She muttered:

'You cannot talk to me like that. You are the guilty one.'

Fiercely indignant, Rosemary turned back to Paul. Every drop of fighting blood in her body was roused now. She was not going to submit to these atrocious accusations. She was going to fight for her honour, for justice, and for Paul, because she loved him.

With burning cheeks, and eyes blazing, she spoke to her husband:

'Listen to me, Paul. As God is my judge, I am absolutely innocent. Mercedes put those powders in my jewel-case. She is responsible for everything. She suggested that wine, and chose the glass for you. As for your cousin, Harry Dyall, I suspect him of being in league with Mercedes. If you made investigations, you would probably find that it was she who met him outside the gates of the villa yesterday. I haven't seen him since we parted near Granada. I tell you, now and here, that I love you, and that I'd give my life for you. I will not be accused of having a lover, or of attempting to get rid of you. I won't even admit such a possibility. I shall behave as though you are all mad. I refuse to leave you or my home.'

Paul, amazed by this outburst, looked at her curiously with his heavy-lidded eyes. Even at this crisis he was struck by the grace and beauty of her. She was wonderful with that light in her eyes, and that violent colour in her cheeks.

'Another thing,' added Rosemary. 'I'm not going to stay here alone to be bullied by all of you. I have sent for Miss Bryant, my best friend, from

London. She shall stay here as my guest. I presume, Paul, that your Spanish courtesy will not permit you to refuse admittance to the only friend I have in the world?'

'I don't care what you do,' he said. 'I only wish to get to the bottom of this frightfulness.'

'Then make your accusations against your cousin Harry, and against Mercedes, rather than hurl your insults at me, your wife,' said Rosemary.

She turned and rushed out of the room. Outside, her violence subsided and left her white and shaken. At Paul's bedside, Mercedes made further attempts to influence Paul against his wife.

He scarcely listened to her. His head ached, and his body felt devitalised. From sheer weakness the moisture rolled in beads down his drawn face. He lay against the pillows, thinking, brooding. He could not banish the memory of his young wife as she had stood there beside him just now, passionately denouncing them all. She was no weakling, certainly, and the fearless streak in him bowed to her courage. It did not seem to him, either, that she had shown much admission of guilt.

'I love you, and I would give my life for you,' she had said. Only once before had she uttered such words, and that was in the Madrid express, when she had lain in his arms.

Was it true that Harry was scheming against him . . . and that Mercedes had planned these evil things?

Rose-Marie had denied that Harry was her lover. And she refused to leave Villa Lucia. It was all a Chinese puzzle, and he could not begin to work it out.

He pressed his finger-tips to his eyeballs. They were burning. He was wracked with doubts, tormented with suspicion, and yet still so much at heart in love with his wife.

Mercedes watched him with her great black eyes, half guessing what passed through his brain. She was afraid that, unless she could set the seal on his disbelief in Rosemary, he might weaken and turn back to her.

The Spanish girl flung herself on one knee beside the bed, seized one of Paul's hands, and covered the beautifully shaped fingers with kisses.

'*Te quiero*, I love thee, *Pablo mio*,' she whispered in their own language.

He drew his hand away. Her amorousness vaguely irritated him in his present mood. He turned from her.

'Leave me, Mercedes; leave me, please. I am not well enough to stand any more.'

'*Pablo*, send that vile English girl away.'

'I am not certain of her guilt.'

'Then you are mad.'

'I am not certain,' he repeated violently. 'And in any case I intend to do nothing until I am out of my bed. Leave me, Mercedes. I refuse to discuss Rose-Marie or this poisoning episode until I have had more time to think.'

She rose, shrugging her shoulders, and walked from the room. She was disappointed. Things had not gone altogether her way. She had hoped at least that Rosemary would be so terrified of Paul, and of disgrace, that she would voluntarily leave Malaga.

Mercedes had not expected her to stand up and fight like this. She must get in touch with Paul's cousin at once, and tell him which way things were going.

Out on the veranda Rosemary lay in a long basket-chair, feeling hot and exhausted, although it was cool here, where the trailing passion flowers made a green shelter from the sun. Her eyes were shut. Her lips were red and dolorous. Now and then her lashes lifted, and she looked down the mountain-side, where the faintest breath of the wind shivered the leaves of the olive-trees and turned them to rippling silver. How blue the sea looked down there in Malaga. It was a beautiful Spanish morning. From the other side of the *hacienda* came the musical tenor of a boy singing while he worked, and now and then she could hear the familiar laughter of Carmenita. Carmenita was happy, and in love, and was going to a Bull Fight on Sunday, with her lover.

Rosemary wondered if everybody in the world was happy except Paul and herself, and vile, unprincipled people like Mercedes and Harry Dyall, who were the cause of most of the evil. She had come out here, longing for Spain. And now the warm, gay country was blotted as though by a perpetual mist of tears.

There were moments when she looked back upon that other Rosemary who had sat at a desk in the offices of Messrs. Tring & Sons, typing through the monotonous dreary hours, and asked herself if it would not have been better had she never left that job, and never changed that life for this one. Certainly she could no longer complain that her existence was full of monotony. It was charged with the most extreme melodrama. It was almost fantastic. A tale of passion and cruelty and love and hatred, of all the emotions wrapped into one.

But in the end, when she had finished questioning herself, she knew that she would not have wiped out this part of her life, no matter how tragic the end. If the very worst happened and she finally left Villa Lucia under a cloud of suspicion, with nothing to look forward to, there was always one thing to look back upon and hold to her heart — the memory of the moments when Paul had loved her and she had climbed in his arms to the very stars.

She knew that Mercedes was trying her best to get her to run away. But flight was an admission of guilt. God knew she was guiltless of *that*. It was almost laughable . . . that she, Rosemary, could be thought guilty of attempted murder.

Mercedes was at the back of it all. But what an enigma it was . . . how incomprehensible that girl who had once wept and wailed at the idea of marrying Don Pablo and had rushed away with Manuel Cadozza!

Rosemary lay back on her cushions, sighing deeply, but her beautiful young face was almost hard.

'I won't give in to them,' she told herself. 'I'll make Paul take back every suspicion. Yes, I'll *make* him believe in me again.'

She did not move from her resting-place on the veranda for the rest of that hot and languorous morning. It was just before lunch that Carmenita came running to her with a fold of pale blue paper . . . a wire for the Doña Rosemary Iballo.

Then Rosemary came to life, and, with a flushed face, read Ida's answer. It was only what she had expected. Dear old Ida was willing to forsake her job and risk her future if her 'lamb' needed her.

'*Leaving for Malaga to-morrow,*' the wire said.

Rosemary crumpled the wire in her hand. And at the thought of that gaunt figure and homely face, and the familiar, friendly personality, the tears came gushing into the eyes of Doña Rosemary Iballo, and poured, unheeded, down her face.

* * *

Don Pablo refused to admit anybody into his room that day. He would not even see his wife. And Mercedes had no better luck when she tried to gain admission. Paul was better in health, but his mood was a queer and sullen one. He wanted to be quiet and to think, and to be influenced by nobody.

The little doctor came and fussed over him, and pronounced him to be well on the road to recovery. He alone saw the master of Villa Lucia that day. And Rosemary was forced to get through the long hours as best she could, and to hide her unhappiness from the servants, who watched and whispered amongst themselves.

The one thing that comforted her was the knowledge that Ida was coming. In this sea of trouble the thought of her friend was like a rock. Once Ida was with her, things would not seem so bad. She would at least have a friend . . . and the very best one . . . at her side.

After lunch she sent a note to Paul, which Pietro took to him. She said:

'I hope you are better. You are never out of my thoughts. For God's sake don't harbour suspicion against me, for you will be committing a terrible error if you do. I won't bother you if you don't want to see me, but please send for me soon. I love you.

ROSE-MARIE.'

Paul sent no answer to this, and Rosemary was left still more miserable and doubting.

She avoided Mercedes as far as possible. She shrank in horror from the very thought of speaking to the Spanish girl. And, rather than share any meals with her, Rosemary had a tray brought to her on the veranda — on the grounds that she had a headache and needed fresh air.

At sundown, on the lowest terrace in the gardens of Villa Lucia, Mercedes, a sombre figure in her black dress, with the black lace mantilla on her head, met and conversed at length with Harry Dyall.

'You see,' she said. 'We are a good way toward gaining our ends, but there is much to be done yet. I haven't seen Pablo since early this morning. He won't see anybody. Neither is he entirely convinced that his wife is guilty.'

'He's a fool,' said Harry.

Harry was sober enough to-day. He had very little money left with which to buy a drink. He had left a trail of debts behind him wherever he went, and he was getting into deeper waters every day. He was smoking a cheap Spanish cigarette, and kept his gaze fixed on the white *hacienda*, which he could just see between the green palms. God, but he wanted this place ... the summer residence of the Iballos . . . and all that vast fortune which lay behind it.

'Damn Paul,' thought Harry. 'Why didn't he die of the poison? He might have died if they hadn't got a doctor on the scene so promptly.'

'And now there is fresh trouble,' said Mercedes, between her small white teeth. 'Your dear Rose-Marie has sent for her English friend — the señorita Bryant.' Mercedes shrugged her shoulders. 'Who and what is she, I do not know. But she will be in our way.'

'Damn,' said Harry again. 'The last thing we want is somebody prowling round on *her* side.'

Mercedes' eyes looked wild and black.

'I hate Rose-Marie so much now that I would do any mortal thing to get her out of Spain.'

'Well, well,' said Harry in a pleasant voice. 'And I hate our dear Paul in much the same fashion. But on the other hand I am intrigued by Rose-Marie. Something can be achieved, surely? I'll think things out. I'm badly in need of money. I don't suppose my cousin is particularly pleased with me at the moment, so I may find myself in gaol in Malaga before I can do anything helpful.'

'No, no. I will see to that. Paul has given me money. You shall have some. I will post it to the Caleta Palace to-night.'

Harry flung his cigarette-end into the bushes.

'Alas, señora, I am no longer a guest in that attractive domicile. I have moved to cheaper quarters . . . I have a room over a café in the Calle Larios . . . two doors from the Spanish Club; you know it? Well, send me some money there, and I shall be grateful, and you can rely on me to do all I can for both you and myself.'

Suddenly Mercedes turned her head and listened intently.

'Ssh! Who is that?'

Harry turned his head. There was the sound of faint footsteps on the white stone stairs which led down to the terrace.

'Someone's coming,' he whispered. Mercedes whispered back:

'I must go. I don't wish to be found talking to you. I'll write to-night.'

She touched his arm lightly in farewell, and slipped away between the palms. She knew a path which she could take whereby she could avoid the terrace steps, and which would lead her back to the *hacienda*.

Harry lit another cigarette, and stood there, watching and waiting, while the sound of footsteps grew louder. There was an ugly dissatisfied look in his eyes.

He half wished he had never taken on this job. It was a dirty business, and, after all, Paul was of his own flesh and blood. But unfortunately he was desperate, and if he couldn't get what he wanted by fair means, now, he would have to resort to foul.

Then he saw the slim figure of a girl in a cream silk dress, with scarlet Moroccan belt, and scarlet sandals on bare white feet. A large hat of Spanish straw sheltered a fair, lovely head from the sun. It was Rosemary. She was followed by a beautiful wolf-hound, which kept close to her heels.

Harry's heart leaped. This was more than he had expected.

The wolf-hound scented a stranger, lifted his graceful head, and growled.

'What is it, Tito?' asked Rosemary. The dog was her special pet. It had been a favourite of Paul's in the past, but ever since Rosemary had become mistress of Villa Lucia the wolf-hound had refused to leave her side.

Tito bounded forward, barking furiously.

Then Harry made his appearance, his face greying as the big dog rushed at him.

'I say, call the damn' dog off! Rosemary, call him off.'

Rosemary stood still. When she saw Paul's cousin her face grew hard as flint. She held out a hand to the dog.

'Down, Tito. Tito . . . come here at once.'

The wolf-hound obeyed, and came

back to heel, wagging his tail. But he continued to sniff and growl suspiciously at Harry.

Harry regained his composure, and bowed with an ironic smile.

'Not a pretty greeting for me, sweetheart.'

Rosemary went white to the lips, then fiery red.

'I don't think I've ever in my life met a man so shameless,' she said in a low voice.

'Why should a man be ashamed of adoring you?'

She shook her head in speechless indignation. Was it possible that this vile creature should be first cousin to Paul? He was a degenerate . . . a throwback . . . and yet, with his attractive face and well-groomed appearance, who could dream that he was so despicable a character?

'And are you enjoying life as much now as you did before you ran away with me?' Harry asked her.

'You will oblige me by leaving Villa

Lucia at once,' she said. 'You have no right in these grounds.'

He put out a deprecating hand.

'Come, come, Rose-Marie, since when have I been forbidden my cousin's house?'

'Paul hasn't the faintest idea what you are like, although I hope soon he will find out.'

'Charming of you!'

'Anyhow, I am mistress of Villa Lucia, and I forbid you to come here. Paul is too ill to deal with you himself.'

He looked at the imperious young figure, and raised his eyebrows.

'We are becoming very Spanish and haughty, aren't we?'

'Get out,' said Rosemary.

'And may I ask why you have changed your tune? You were very friendly with me when I came to Villa Lucia last. You asked for my help, and I gave it. You are not very grateful.'

'I've nothing to be grateful to you for. I hadn't the faintest idea what you were like when I accepted your help.'

'And pray what am I like?'

Rosemary shivered a little.

'God knows. I wouldn't like to say. I only know that you're a vile traitor to Paul, and that you're helping Mercedes . . . and that both of you tried to *kill* him last night.'

The muscles of Harry's face tautened. But his eyes, slightly bloodshot, drooped before Rosemary's clear, accusing gaze.

'That's rubbish, of course, and quite unfounded.'

'It's what I believe.'

'The Señora Cadozza tells me otherwise.'

'I won't discuss it with you. You aren't capable of telling the truth.'

'Don't be a little fool. I've no wish whatsoever to kill my cousin. You're being melodramatic. My only wish is to have enough to live on comfortably, and for you to live with me.'

'I honestly think you're mad.'

'Perhaps you'll think otherwise of me when Paul turns you out of his house,' said Harry, with a twisted smile. 'Only remember, you can always come to me.'

She made a gesture of disgust.

'I wouldn't if I were starving. And I'm going to tell Paul that you are at the bottom of all our troubles.'

He caught her wrist in a grip that hurt.

'You'd better be careful what you say, or . . .'

'Or what? Are you afraid of me? . . .' She flung off his hand. 'Are you afraid that Paul might believe *me* for a change?'

Harry put a finger inside his collar and loosened it. Sweat was pouring from his forehead. He wiped it away, then looked Rosemary up and down in an insulting fashion.

'I can afford to wait. I don't think Paul will believe you altogether. I know him. He has a very jealous nature. And you'll find it difficult to get back his faith.'

'Please go.'

'Haven't you a kinder word for me?'

'No.'

He gave an ugly laugh.

'Not even a farewell embrace?'

'Get out of these grounds.'

'I'll have my kiss first,' he said insolently; caught her, before she could move, and kissed her on the mouth.

The wolf-hound seemed to sense that his mistress was struggling against this stranger. He snarled and jumped upon Harry. The next instant the man felt a sharp pain in his arm. With a cry he released Rosemary.

'Damn your b — y dog — he's bitten me.'

Rosemary drew back, trembling, and wiped her lips with a wisp of lace and cambric.

'I hope he has . . . you beast!'

Tito would have sprung at Harry again, but she took his collar and held him off.

'If you enter Villa Lucia again, I'll tell Tito to go for your throat,' Rosemary said, between her teeth.

She turned and walked away, followed by the animal. Harry was left swearing roundly. When he took off his coat and rolled back his shirt-sleeve he found that the wolf-hound had drawn blood. In terror of rabies — for there was much in this country — Harry hastened from the villa and back to Malaga. The sooner a doctor cauterised the place, the better.

Thoroughly sick at heart, Rosemary returned to the *hacienda*.

She felt utterly lonely and depressed. If only Paul would see her . . . if only she could make him understand what was going on!

She sent another message, just before dinner, to Paul's room.

'Please see me for a few minutes . . . you must!'

The answer was sent back:

'I would rather not.'

Then Rosemary took matters into her own hands. Her very love for her husband gave her courage. She was not going to be treated like this . . . kept from Paul's room as though she were in disgrace.

She changed into evening dress, and then, deliberately, walked into Paul's bedroom without knocking.

It was a big severe room, furnished in rather heavy Spanish style with old, massive walnut. But there were priceless rugs on the polished floor and modern curtains of beautiful plum-coloured silk drawn across the tall windows. Paul lay in the big carved bedstead which had belonged to his father, with only a single blanket and a thin silk spread over him. The evening was close, almost stifling, and there was thunder in the air. A single lamp burned beside his bed. He was sitting up, writing.

He raised his head as the door opened, and saw, with astonishment, the figure of his wife.

For an instant he said nothing. She shut the door and came slowly towards him. Sullenly he regarded her.

'I told you I didn't want to see you,'

he said, in a rough voice.

'You had no right to send me such a message. I want to see you, and I'm here,' was her reply.

He curved one narrow dark brow ironically. She was learning to stand up to life, this English girl. But, then, there had always been spirit in her . . . astonishing spirit in that fragile delicate body. To look at her, and without knowing her, one might imagine that she was gentle, timid, easily terrorised. But from the beginning she had proved herself otherwise. She was a passionate lover and a brave fighter. The same reckless courage that had made her take Mercedes' place at the altar rails, led her now, to defy him.

He was secretly pleased. All day he had been thinking about her, and with every moment he was becoming more convinced of her innocence. He did not trust that dark-eyed, stealthy Spanish girl. She was an amorous kitten with sharp claws . . . and fast growing into a dangerous cat. She was not to be trusted. He half believed that she was at the bottom of the whole dastardly plot. On the other hand he was not sufficiently convinced that Rose-Marie was innocent, to surrender to her . . . yet.

He even sneered at her when she was close to his bedside.

'You make yourself cheap . . . coming where you are not wanted.'

She flushed scarlet, but held her head high.

'No matter what you have against me, I don't think you can accuse me of that . . . unless you wish to remind me of the Madrid express . . . which you are so fond of doing.'

He gave a short laugh, and laid his fountain-pen and block aside. Critically he examined her with his dark, narrow gaze.

She wore white to-night . . . a white chiffon dress of exquisite severity, with a square neck and long tight sleeves. A single diamond cross hung from her neck, and glittered on her bosom. She was very pale, and her eyes were shadowy. With her fair hair brushed smoothly behind her ears and curled at the nape of her neck, she made a figure of amazing pride and of a chaste beauty that fired Don Pablo's imagination. She was almost nunlike standing there in that white chiffon dress. And, when she stirred, the diamond cross caught fire against the milky curve of the lovely breast. Damnation . . . but she was so proudly beautiful to-night, he wanted to fall at her feet and kiss her ankles and worship her. He knew that he could change that snow to fire, and that in his arms that nun-like figure would be transformed into a warm, clinging woman. He had done it so many times. He wanted her madly now that he saw her. It seemed to him years rather than days since he had touched her lips with his. And even those lips needed colour . . . his Rose-Marie had not used much make-up to-night. Perhaps it was a trick . . . all this ice and purity.

'Are you better?' she asked.

'Yes.'

'Is there anything I can do for you?'

'You have done enough. You half killed me.'

She winced but kept her head held high.

'That isn't true, and you know it. I repeat what I said to you this morning. I am absolutely innocent.'

He dragged his gaze from her. Her loveliness was an enchantment which he wished to escape.

'I think,' he said coldly, 'when I am up, to-morrow, I shall leave Villa Lucia. You can remain. You can have my cousin here, or a dozen other lovers.'

She caught her lower lip between her teeth. That hurt, and it was meant to do, and he was amused when he saw the swift colour flame to her cheeks and thoat.

'How dare you say that? And why — why should you believe Mercedes Cadozza and not me?'

'I believe nobody,' he said sullenly. 'I only want to get away from all of you.'

'I thought at least that you knew the meaning of justice.'

He turned to her quickly.

'And would it be unjust of me to get out and leave you with everything?'

'I don't want to be left with everything. I only want you to believe in me.'

'And why this sudden *penchant* for me?' he sneered. 'You've spent so many months telling me that you hated me.'

'Yes' — she nodded and pressed her hands together, her rapid heart-beats hurting her — 'but it was agreed that there should be peace between us. I told you that I . . . that I had found that I loved you.'

'And I toasted the peace with poison,' he said darkly.

She caught one of his nervous hands with hers.

'My God, you know that it wasn't I who put that poison in the glass, Paul. You *must* believe me. The whole thing is a plot. I keep telling you . . . your cousin Harry is a vile scoundrel. He wants your money, and Mercedes wants you. They're both trying to get me out of it. Can't you, won't you, believe it?'

He stirred restlessly, moving his head from side to side like a caged, maddened thing. He was caged by his own dark suspicions and doubts of her. Yet the touch of her hand made him shudder with bitter ecstasy.

'That sounds feasible, but I have only your word for it.'

'You shall have proof, if you wait and watch.'

'Leave me,' he said, panting. The moisture was running down his pale, handsome face. He was still weak, unfit for excessive emotion. 'Don't torture me with all this now.'

But Rosemary was fighting for everything that she held dear. Suddenly the proud figure of ice seemed to thaw and break. She knelt down and pressed her lips against his hand. Another woman had done that recently . . . Mercedes . . . and it had irritated him. But the touch of Rosemary's velvet mouth against his fingers was not an irritation . . . it was an invitation which he found it difficult to refuse. And it was such an unusual thing to see that fair head bowed . . . to witness her submission to him . . . her complete surrender.

'Paul; Paul,' she breathed. 'Tell me that you believe in me. Don't send me away. I love you so . . . oh, I mean it. And if you'll only give me a chance . . . '

She broke off, choking, and looked up at him. Don Pablo stared into the golden eyes which were liquid with tears and felt himself weakening, drowning.

Madre de Dios, but she was the one and only woman on earth who could make him weaken like this . . . turn his very blood to water . . . render him like clay in her slender hands. He was almost ashamed of such weakness. He wanted her, and yet could not bear that his reason should be overruled by his emotions, and that is what he feared might happen now.

He drew his hand away from her

clinging fingers, from her lips.

'I can't think . . . I can't breathe,' he said.

'You would be much better outside,' she said with a breathless laugh. 'It's stifling in here. The doctor advised you to take fresh air. Will you let me order the car — the little one that I can drive? It's a wonderful night. There's no wind. Let me take you up there in the mountains where we can be alone and talk . . . '

Her personality swamped him. He felt, suddenly, like wax in her hands. He, too, wanted to get out . . . away with her . . . away from the villa and from Mercedes, from the world. To be alone with his Rose-Marie where he could listen and believe.

He flung off the bed-clothes. His whole body seemed to be electrified . . . brimming with new life.

'Yes, I'll come,' he said. 'Ring for Pietro . . . order your car.'

Hope surged anew through her veins. With a feeling of intoxication she rang the bell and left him. Five minutes later he was dressed, wrapped in a warm coat, and downstairs, where she awaited him in the small car which he had taught her to drive. She had put a soft mink coat over her white velvet gown. Her fair head was bare. She looked radiant.

'*Venga!* Come!' she said to him in Spanish. 'Come and let's talk and understand each other, *Pablo mio.*'

He took his place beside her.

'If I could only believe you,' he said. 'If I could only be made to understand . . . '

Mercedes came out of the villa, and ran down the steps to the car. She had seen everything, and she was seething with rage and disappointment. But she played her last card — a card suggested by Harry Dyall.

She gave Paul a letter. The envelope was stamped and addressed to the Doña Rosemary. The flap was torn open as though the letter had been read.

'Rose-Marie has just dropped this in the hall, from her bag,' she said to Paul sweetly.

Rosemary said: 'What is that, Paul?'

He put the letter in his coat pocket, without looking at it.

'Oh, only something you dropped. Drive on . . . quickly . . . for heaven's sake let us get away from the *hacienda*, while this mood is on us.'

She did not suspect treachery then. She had no idea what that letter was. It might be an old one from Ida for all she knew. She had no interest in it, anyhow. She only wanted to take Paul out on the starlit mountain slopes, and use all her woman's wiles to win him back. Yes, she was sheer woman . . . possessive, primitive, fighting for her lover.

The warm air beat softly against their faces as the little car hummed along the winding road and climbed upwards, upwards, towards the very stars. Something in Rosemary's heart sang. She could feel Paul's warm body vibrating against hers.

'He's mine, he's all mine,' she thought exultantly. 'He *must* love me to-night . . . he must believe in me.'

When they had climbed a thousand feet, Rosemary brought the car to a standstill, and switched off the engine. They sat side by side, without touching each other. The night was unbelievably beautiful. The stars glittered in millions over their heads. Far, far below, the lights of Malaga twinkled . . . and points of light, like pin-pricks from one or two fishing-boats on the sea, winking in the night.

Rosemary took off her coat and flung her arms above her head.

'Oh, Paul,' she whispered. 'We're absolutely alone . . . here, away from the world.'

He looked at her, swayed by her beauty and by the romance of the mountain heights.

'Rose-Marie, if only I could believe!'

'You can, Paul, if you try.'

'I don't know . . . all these horrible things . . .'

'Are nothing to do with me,' she finished quickly. And swiftly she turned her slim body and flung herself into his arms, crushing the delicate chiffon dress, locking her arms about his throat.

'Paul, my darling, you *must* believe in me! I tell you it is Mercedes who is responsible for that dreadful business . . . the poison in your wine. Mercedes who is at the bottom of it all — *and* Harry Dyall. I love you, Paul. I love you. Please listen to *me*, not to them. Let's go away from Spain, from everybody, and begin again — just you and I. You can see for yourself, I want only you, and nobody else on earth.'

Doubt lingered a few seconds in the man's brain. Then feverishly he took her, embraced her. He buried his lips in her hair.

'I want to love you again. There has never been any woman but you . . . '

'Kiss me,' she said, and lifted a rapt, beautiful face to his. 'There has never been any man in my life but you.'

Their lips met in a long deep kiss. And, when that kiss ended, he covered her hands with kisses.

'Oh, Rose-Marie, my wife, my love,' he said, in his own ardent language. 'I love thee. *Te quiero — siempre — always.*'

She looked up at him with shining eyes.

'Let's stay here . . . under the stars,' she whispered.

'I shall never leave you again,' he whispered.

'Tell me you believe in me.'

'I do believe — yes, yes, I do. How could you kiss me so . . . thrill so to my kiss . . . if you loved any other man?'

He smoothed the fair soft hair back from her forehead.

'How beautiful you are, my Rose-Marie.'

The letter Mercedes had handed him slipped from the pocket of his coat, and fell on to Rosemary's lap . . . lay there like a small white snake that had wriggled into the Garden of Eden.

Rosemary did not notice it.

'Paul,' she whispered.

But he gazed at the letter. He had recognised his cousin Harry's handwriting. It was Harry who had written that letter to Rosemary. Slowly Paul lifted it up and handed it to his wife.

'This note,' he said in a queer voice. 'Will you read it to me . . . tell me what my cousin has to say to you?'

Rosemary lifted the letter and turned it slowly over and over. Her brows contracted. She looked at Paul in a puzzled way.

'This note? I don't know what it is. Mercedes gave it to you just before we left, didn't she?'

'Yes,' said Paul, his eyes fixed on her. 'She said you dropped it in the hall.'

'Did I?' said Rosemary smiling. 'Then I can't imagine what it is.'

Paul tapped the white envelope in her hand. 'It is addressed to you, Rose-Marie, and it has been opened.'

She stared down at it. 'But not by me.'

Suspicion leapt into Paul's jealous mind again. Rosemary watched the tender passion of his beautifully shaped mouth harden to that thin, cruel line which she dreaded.

'Rose-Marie, this letter is from my cousin Harry. Why is Harry writing to you?'

'I don't know, honestly . . . Paul, darling, are we going to let this wretched letter spoil everything? Paul, we were so marvellously happy just now and — '

'May I see that letter?' His voice cut like a whip across her tender voice.

She hesitated. She began to sense evil. Somewhere there had been foul play again. And, of course, Mercedes — that wretched, unscrupulous girl — was at the bottom of it, with her spite, her greed, her bitter jealousy.

Rosemary lifted her chin with a proud little movement.

'Very well, Paul. Here is the letter. I don't know what's in it. I give you my word on that.'

He took the envelope, and drew a thin sheet of foreign paper from it. It took him only a few seconds to scan what was written in Harry's bold, slanting hand!

'MY ROSE-MARIE [that name was sufficient to make Paul grit his teeth in fury], — *How long can we bear this intolerable position? When will you come to me? You've said so often that you love me — that you hate and fear Paul. Don't be afraid. Leave him and join me in England. Our plans failed . . . but we'll defeat him yet. I live to hold you in my arms again, and to feel your wonderful, maddening lips respond to mine as they did last time we met. I kiss your feet. Your devoted lover,* — HARRY.'

Paul read this passionate note once. His dark eyes blazed. He trembled in every limb.

'It looks as though you know nothing of it. Oh, my God, it looks like it. You

. . . you . . . ' He broke off, as though he could find no word to express his horror and indignation

Rosemary stared at the letter, then read it quickly. She managed to take in the meaning of those incriminating words. Of course it was Harry Dyall and Mercedes again. Rosemary's blood boiled.

'Paul, this is the first time I've set eyes on this horrible letter. Someone else opened it. Mercedes. Harry must have written it on purpose, and given it to her. It's a plot. A wicked plot. Don't you see? Don't you understand?'

He put up a hand. He was still shaking.

'No, I can't say I do. My cousin *is* your lover. I was suspicious before . . . when you left the villa with him and went to that Fonda. Mercedes says she has seen you together, frequently. He calls you Rose-Marie. I thought only *I* gave you that name. He says you hate and fear me . . . he intimates that you and *he* contrived to get rid of me the other night. Great God, the frightfulness of it. And you dared to kiss me to-night, to smile at me.'

'Stop!' broke in Rosemary. 'It's all grossly unfair. This letter was written on purpose to incriminate me. Paul, Paul, don't be so blind. Can't you see that those two want to separate us?'

Paul shook off her hand. Sheer, primitive jealousy consumed him. He looked at her in horror. This time, he told himself, furiously, he would never believe in her or any living woman again.

'Go to your Harry,' he said. 'Go to him. You two would have murdered me if you could. Go and be happy in that knowledge. Oh, my God.'

He turned from her. A terrible weakness seized him. The sweat broke out over his body. He was far from strong yet. The terrific emotion of this night and the reaction setting in now were too much for him.

His head drooped. He lay back in the car. With terror in her heart Rosemary caught his hands.

'Paul; Paul; oh, *Paul*!'

He tried to speak, to push away her hand, then drifted into insensibility.

For a full minute she went on calling his name, wildly, chafing his hands.

His faint seemed long and serious. Nothing she could do revived him.

She switched on the engine, and drove down the mountain road, back to Villa Lucia. Jumping out of the car, she ran up the steps, through the veranda, into the *hacienda*. She rang a bell feverishly for the servants. Two men came running in answer.

'Your master is in the car — he has fainted,' she said. 'Carry him in, up to his bed, and telephone at once for the doctor.'

The men bowed, and hastened to do her bidding.

While they carried in Paul's unconscious figure, Rosemary stood by, watching with a heart that sank lower every moment. In agony of anxiety, she looked at her husband's pale face. She wondered if this thing had been his death-blow — if he would die of it. If so, she wanted to die too.

She looked at her wrist-watch, and saw that it was late. She and Paul must have been up there on the mountain-side for some hours. Then Mercedes came running down the stairs — Mercedes in a silken wrapper, dark eyes snapping with excitement.

Rosemary looked at Mercedes in speechless reproach.

'Ah,' said Mercedes slowly. 'So you make another attempt on Pablo's life? And this time, if he dies, a successful one. But, if he dies, the police shall know that . . .'

'Be quiet,' broke in Rosemary. 'Don't dare go on, you wicked, wicked girl. I wonder you are not stricken dead where you stand for uttering all those frightful lies. That abominable letter from Paul's cousin . . . which you gave him . . . that is what has nearly killed him to-night.'

Mercedes dropped her gaze nervously, but she managed to laugh.

'I'm not going to listen to your ravings. You ought to pack your things and get out ... get back where you belong. You have no right in this *hacienda*.'

Rosemary gave Mercedes a lightning look, then turned and walked upstairs.

She entered Paul's bedroom. He lay on his pillows. Pietro had undressed him, and was bathing his brow with eau-de-Cologne. Rosemary saw, to her immense relief, that Paul was conscious now. His eyes were open. But he was still ghastly pale. When he saw Rosemary's slim lovely figure, he started up in bed and pushed the valet away.

'Leave my room,' he said, in a violent tone, to his wife.

Rosemary came nearer, her cheeks and throat burning red.

'Paul, for God's sake ... listen ... be calm ... '

'Go,' he said, in a smothered voice. 'And leave Villa Lucia, too. I never want to see you again.'

'Paul; Paul; won't you listen to me? I

swear by all that I hold sacred that this is a plot against me.'

'I don't believe you. Go to Harry. *Go*, I say!'

Rosemary flung herself on her knees beside him.

'Paul; Paul; you're breaking my heart. Can't you believe?'

'No. I'm through . . . done with you,' he said. He looked down at the fair head so close to his own, and shuddered. 'I never want to see you again. Go with Harry, and I will divorce you — set you free.'

Silence. Rosemary's heart seemed to stand still. Through a hot mist she stared at him. Then slowly she rose to her feet. She said, in a slow voice: 'Aren't you going to give me a chance to prove that I'm innocent, Paul?'

'You can't. How can you? It's obvious you are guilty.'

'Yes, things look black. I know it. Yet if you loved me . . . '

'I did love you!' he broke in. 'I adored you . . . every hair of your head, every feature of your face. I wanted you always for my wife — for the mother of my sons — and you've betrayed me . . . from first to last you've betrayed me . . . from the time you took poor Mercedes' place in the cathedral, that day . . . to to-night . . . when you tore up the last roots of my faith . . . with Harry's letter.'

Another silence. Rosemary felt so full of despair, she could only stand there, staring down at him.

She felt that it was indeed the end. She had fought hard for Paul's love and for her own rights. She had refused to be beaten by Harry, Mercedes, by Paul himself. And now there seemed no hope. Her hope was dead. There was no fight left in her. Between them all, they had defeated her at last. She said, under her breath:

'So you . . . really believe the very worst of me? Very well, Paul. It *is* the end for us. I'll go. Good-bye.'

She turned and moved toward the bedroom door. She walked like one whose feet were leaden. Paul's feverish handsome eyes followed her uneasily. He said: 'Why not admit what you've done before you go? You'll join Harry now, of course.'

Then Rosemary turned. The bitter reproach and pain in the look she gave him haunted Don Pablo for many hours and days to follow.

'No, Paul. I shall not join Harry. Harry and Mercedes are responsible for all this dreadful business. I shall go back to England. You can divorce me if you choose, although never for a single moment have I been disloyal. And I shall admit nothing, because I have nothing to admit. I'm absolutely innocent. Good-bye.'

She walked out of the room and closed the door.

Paul lay back on his pillows, panting, battling with the sudden desire to call her back. Never to see her again. His Rose-Marie, his beautiful wife, that was frightful! And she protested her innocence; her loyalty to the end. Oh God,

God, why didn't he know the truth.

But she had gone. And he did not call her back.

Like a slim dark shadow, Mercedes, in her silken wrapper, crept into his room and came to his bedside. She looked down at him with passionate eyes.

'*Pablo mio,*' she said, in her own language, 'are you better?'

'Yes,' he said dully.

'You should be easier in your mind, also, now that wicked woman has gone,' said Mercedes. 'She is packing . . . preparing to leave the villa.'

He looked up at the girl, with lustreless eyes.

'Do not speak of her, Mercedes.'

Mercedes concealed a little smile of triumph. She bent over him, and boldly laid a kiss on his brow.

'You are safe now . . . with one who truly loves you, *querido mio,*' she whispered.

But he shivered under her kiss and waved her away. 'Leave me, please.'

'You must forget her now, Pablo.'

'Forget her?' he echoed. 'That won't be possible, my dear.'

'She is not worth remembering. And your cousin, Harry, is a wicked man. He is here, outside, waiting to take her to Rome.'

Paul ground his teeth.

'Great God, why do you torture me? . . . Leave me!' he said, and turned his face to the pillow.

Mercedes could not get another word out of him. But she left the room, confident that Rosemary's downfall was complete.

7

In her luxurious bedroom, the young Doña Rosemary moved like an automaton, packing her clothes. This was the end of Rose-Marie, wife of Don Pablo. The end of all happiness. The last piece of despicable treachery on the part of Harry Dyall and Mercedes had ended everything. She could not expect Paul to believe in her now. And she was tired, so tired of the whole disastrous affair that she was almost glad that it was all over.

In a distraught way she put together her clothes, only a few, and the most simple. She would leave her beautiful, expensive wardrobe, and, of course, all the Iballo jewels, behind her. She was so exhausted bodily and mentally that she hardly knew how to get through these next few hours. But she had made up her mind to leave Villa Lucia. Never again in this world would she plead with Paul.

And then, suddenly, in the midst of the feverish packing, she remembered that Ida was coming . . . it was too late to stop her. The telegraphic service between Spain and England was most unreliable, and, if she wired first thing to-morrow morning, the wire might not be received in England for twenty-four hours. By that time Miss Bryant would be well on her way.

Rosemary sat on the edge of her bed, a pile of stockings in her lap, and stared at them in a helpless way. What a hopeless position! She did not want to stay here any longer. She could not bear the thought. But there seemed no alternative, until Ida arrived. Then she would have to explain the whole horrible story, and, of course, she and Ida would return to England together. Her heart sank at the prospect. Now that she was growing calmer and could think more clearly she was beginning to see all the difficulties ahead . . .

difficulties she could scarcely bear to dwell upon. There was the question of money . . . she had nothing in the world of her own. She would be forced to ask Paul for the fare home . . . and for Ida's fare, too. And Ida had lost her job . . . through her. How ghastly! They would both arrive back in London, and have to search for new jobs, unless Messrs. Tring & Sons took one or the other of them back, and that was rather more than could be expected.

Rosemary covered her eyes with her hand, and shook her head wearily. The struggle was becoming too much for her. And she realised, half ashamed, that she would loathe the old existence of pinching and scraping. She had grown accustomed to the beauty and comfort of her life here in Spain. Apart from her agonising love for Paul, and what it would mean to lose him for ever, it would not be easy suddenly to cease being Doña Rosemary Iballo and become Rosemary Wallace, typist, again.

She looked at the big gold bed with

the dim Moorish lamp burning over it, at the creamy satin sheets embroidered with the Iballo crest, the wonderful spread woven with rich threads of gold and jade and old rose. She thought, with a terrible pang, of the smooth dark head which had so often rested against those pillows. And suddenly she flung herself across it, her body shaken with weeping.

'Oh, my God, my God!' she whispered. 'How unfair it is. Paul; Paul; I've loved you so!'

It seemed to her a night of grey desolation. When Carmenita came with her breakfast-tray, Rosemary was still there, her clothes in chaos all over the room, and she, half dressed, lying across the bed.

The little Spanish maid, who had grown deeply attached to her young English mistress, was shocked beyond words. She drew the curtains, and let the warm sunlight flood the room, then hastened to Rosemary's side.

'*Doña mia*, you are ill? You would

like the doctor?'

Rosemary, more dead than alive, looked at her with lack-lustre eyes.

'I feel a little ill. My head burns.'

'*Oiga!* You have a fever!' exclaimed Carmenita. touching one of Rosemary's hot wrists. 'You must get to bed, and I will send for the *medico*.'

But Rosemary declined the doctor's aid. She had, perhaps, a touch of fever, but she knew that her illness was of the mind rather than of the body. She was completely done up . . . incapable of further thought or action. The disastrous finale to all her hopes concerning Paul had been too much for her.

Half an hour later she was in bed, burning, aching from head to foot. Carmenita fussed over her, gave her aspirin, sat beside the bed, rubbing her temples with eau-de-Cologne.

Rosemary felt almost too ill to care what happened . . . or to mind what Paul was doing or thinking. But she sent a message by the maid . . . managed to open her eyes, half blinded by headache, and scribble a note. It told Paul that she was ill and in bed, and to-morrow night she expected her friend from England, and that when she came they would return to London together.

Paul, not much better than Rosemary, had insisted upon getting up to-day. The note was given him when he sat in a chair on the veranda, staring moodily at the garden. He, too, was in that condition of mind when he cared very little what happened. He only wanted to end the whole hideous affair. He had taken it for granted, from what Mercedes told him, that Rosemary was leaving Villa Lucia at once . . . with Harry.

When he read her note he shrugged his shoulders and handed it to the Spanish girl who sat beside him. She was not leaving him alone any more than she could help.

Mercedes, too, shrugged her shoulders.

'My lady is not in a hurry to leave her

comfortable home.'

'Let her stay,' was Paul's indifferent reply. 'She means nothing to me. I am only waiting until I am strong enough, and then I go to Biarritz. If I have any more of this it will kill me.'

'And what of me?' Mercedes asked, giving him an expressive look from her large black eyes.

Again he shrugged his shoulders. He felt a dead thing . . . nothing, nobody, could move him to a single emotion. But in a vague way he pitied his country-woman. He said:

'Don't be afraid. I'll provide for you.'

Mercedes said no more, but she thought much. It would not satisfy her to be just 'provided for'. She made up her mind that she would go with Don Pablo when he left Malaga for Biarritz.

She managed, later in the day, to communicate with Harry. She took Paul's car, on the pretext of wanting to do some shopping in Malaga, and met Harry in the Spanish Club.

'The letter was a wonderful success

indeed,' Mercedes congratulated him. 'But we are not through the wood yet. Rosemary is ill in bed, and unable to leave Villa Lucia, and this friend of hers is arriving . . . I am afraid of the friend, frankly.'

Harry was optimistic.

'This Bryant woman can't do anything. Don't worry. Rosemary is so far compromised now that nothing can save her. And, in case of emergency, she could always be compromised a little further, yes?'

When Mercedes left him to return to the villa she was almost as optimistic as Harry himself, and in the best of humours. But she got very little satisfaction from the time she spent with Don Pablo during the rest of that day. He was in one of his black moods, and refused, definitely, to discuss his wife. So far as Harry was concerned, he had only one thing to say . . . he had written to his lawyers and instructed them to cut Harry Dyall out of his will.

This piece of news Mercedes did not

intend to convey to Harry. It might have a disastrous effect on him. He might come here, make a fuss, and involve her, Mercedes.

★   ★   ★

Don Pablo waited for his strength to return, and Rosemary, shut in her room, was nursed by Carmenita, her faithful little maid — the only person, Rosemary felt, in Villa Lucia, who cared whether she lived or died.

She clung now with pathetic eagerness to the thought that Ida Bryant was coming.

Then came the afternoon when that worthy lady made her appearance at Villa Lucia. It was quite a spectacular arrival. Rosemary, who was up and at her bedroom window, saw it. Ida, sitting in the back of an open taxi, her hat on the back of her head, several small parcels and a travelling bag clasped to her bosom, her feet on her trunk, and a violent altercation going on between her and the driver, neither of them understanding a word the other said.

Ida's plain face was crimson with indignation and heat. Rosemary could hear the word 'robber' issuing shrilly from her lips. In the midst of her despair she had to smile. And afterwards she heard the story from Ida. When the smiling Spaniard had seized her things at the station, she had taken it for granted that he was going to steal them; she was convinced that she was in the land of thieves, and that the country was even more barbaric than she had anticipated.

Ida stepped from the taxi. The driver descended from his seat and demanded his money. They shouted at each other for a moment. Then Rosemary leaned out of her window and called down:

'Ida! Darling, don't bother . . . I'll send my maid down to settle with him.'

Ida, in process of shaking her umbrella at the protesting Spaniard, looked up, and immediately radiated smiles.

'Rosemary! My *lamb*!'

'Come up quickly,' said Rosemary.

And she turned from the window and sat down again, her knees shaking under her. She was still weak from the recent fever, and already, at the first glimpse of her friend, in tears.

In the beautiful hall of Villa Lucia, Ida, still clutching some of her smaller baggage, collided with the tall figure of Paul. He drew back with an apology, and stared, astonished. He disliked plain and dowdy women, and this one was definitely the plainest and dowdiest who had ever had entrance to Villa Lucia. He cast an appalled glance at her hat, her untidy hair, her scarlet face, the crumpled dress of crêpe de Chine which had seen better days, her large feet in their cheap black shoes. He said:

'Good God, who are you?'

'Thank the lord you can speak the king's English!' she explained. 'I've heard nothing but these barbaric Spaniards howling at me for the last two days. And I'm sick to death of it. I thought I was going to be murdered when I crossed Madrid. Not a Cook's man to be seen. Nobody who could understand a word I said! What a country!'

Paul did not lack a sense of humour, and his pale handsome face suddenly relaxed into a faint smile. What an odd creature. One couldn't really grace her by the name of woman. She was just an oddity.

'I regret that you find my country so primitive,' he said.

'*Your* country! Are you Spanish?'

'I am.'

'Then I wonder you don't spit at my feet. I've seen enough spitting to last me for years, and heard it!'

Ida grimaced, and shook herself all over.

Again Paul smiled. 'There *are* civilised members of the community in my country.'

'Are you by any chance . . . why . . . I do believe you're Rosemary's husband, aren't you?'

The smile froze on Paul's lips. He bowed, and clicked his heels together.

'I am Don Pablo.'

'Well, now, isn't that nice,' she said, beaming, and held out a hand. 'I'm Romie's friend, Miss Bryant.'

Paul did not take the hand but bowed again. 'How do you do,' he said, in an icy voice, then turned sharply and left her standing there.

She gaped after him. Well, that wasn't very pretty! Really, this country was full of madmen. If they didn't spit, they were rude in some other way.

'Thank God I'm English,' said Ida, with patriotic fervour, then turned and called loudly: 'Rosemary!'

'Come up!' came the reply.

Ida went up the stairs, slipping a little on the smooth marble. What a house! It was like a museum. Beautiful, perhaps, but all very lavish and spectacular. But she would have preferred to have seen Rosemary in a nice English home furnished by Maples.

Then, when she entered Rosemary's

286

beautiful golden bedroom, she saw nothing but the familiar and beloved figure of the girl herself. Rosemary, in a white lace *négligée*, with arms out-stretched. Ida took her into a fervent embrace.

'*Lamb!* How lovely!'

But the next moment her pleasure had turned to astonishment and dismay, for Rosemary was sobbing, like one broken-hearted, in her arms. And, when she had time to collect her scattered thoughts and look at her friend, her critical eyes saw that Rosemary was ill, almost as white as her laces. This was not the glowing, sunburned creature whom she had expected to find, nor the happy wife which Rosemary's letters had led her to believe. This was a changed Rosemary, altogether baffling to the honest Ida, and there was a broken look in those hazel eyes which horrified her.

'Why, my dear child!' said Ida, drawing her friend down on to the edge of the bed, still holding her hands. 'What on earth has happened? Something ghastly, I can see. Why, you look as though you've been through hell.'

Rosemary dried her eyes. Her fair head drooped.

'I think that describes it. I *have* been through hell.'

Ida flung off her hat.

'Tell me everything. Thank the Lord I've come. I knew it! I knew I wasn't far wrong when I said you'd regret it if you came to this outlandish country and married one of these savage Spaniards.'

Rosemary hadn't a smile left, but she gave a short, miserable laugh.

'It isn't altogether because of the man I've married . . . nor is it anything to do with the country. My troubles are due to a Spanish girl, who is not only barbaric but mad! And largely, also, to an Englishman, I'm afraid; so don't run away with the idea that it's all the fault of Spain, Ida.'

'I must know everything.'

'It's a long, long story, and a pretty

ghastly one. You'd better have a wash and a change first, and some food.'

'I don't want anything but a glass of lemonade.'

'You can soon have that.' Rosemary pressed the bell to summon Carmenita. 'Or would you like a nice English cup of tea? I've taught my maid how to make that.'

'That would be heavenly,' said Ida, as though she had been away from England two years instead of two days.

'I met your husband in the hall,' she added, and pursed her lips. 'I can't say he was over pleased to see me.'

Rosemary closed her eyes. 'I don't suppose he was.'

'But I thought you adored each other.'

Rosemary gave a little moan. 'Oh, Ida, I did adore him! I still do, that's the worst of it, and I think he might have adored me if it hadn't been for that vile, insane girl whom he let into this house.'

'So he's *that* sort of man!' The

darkest thoughts immediately leapt into Ida's mind.

Rosemary laughed and wept together.

'No, no, it isn't what you think! If it were only that sort of thing, how easy it would be! But it's far more complicated and terrible! And so much of it is my own fault. When your tea comes, I'll tell you everything. I won't spare myself. I know a good deal of it is due to my own folly. And then, when you've heard, you can judge, and you will agree with me that it wasn't altogether my fault that it's turned out such a failure.'

Ida was prepared to agree with Rosemary long before the story started. And once it was told, over the cup of tea — Ida had four — she sat there in a sort of stupefied silence, staring at her friend, her homely face a little paler now that the flush of heat and effort had faded.

For some while she could not altogether credit the truth. It seemed preposterous, fantastic, and much more like a wild film than anything. But

Rosemary convinced her of the truth of it. The thing became reality for Ida. And the deeper it all soaked into her mind, the more furiously indignant she became on Rosemary's behalf.

Of course, Romie had been mad to take the place of the Spanish girl in the first place. How had she dared? . . . just fancy dressing up in those wedding clothes and doing such a thing! But Don Pablo had been a wicked brute to keep her to it and force her to stay here as his wife. Yes, he was a cruel brute, and he looked it, in spite of his handsome face. But the rest of the story was even more abominable. How dared that wicked Spanish girl come back and play these nasty tricks? How dared the cousin interfere? As for the poison, the attempted murder, and all this business about Rosemary having Harry for her lover, Ida had never heard such outrageous things in her life. No matter how much Rosemary blamed herself, Ida wasn't going to blame her. But call her a little fool for ever wanting to stay here, she did. She ought to have packed up and come home long ago.

'Why on earth didn't you?' Ida demanded.

Then the girl looked at her with tragic eyes, and said: 'Because I loved him.'

'Gawd!' said Ida, under her breath. 'You're a bit of a puzzle to me. If any man treated me like that I'd lay an umbrella across his head.'

At the thought of Ida laying an umbrella across Paul's head, Rosemary had to laugh again, but the laughter ended in tears. She wept against Ida's shoulder.

'But I do love him, even if you can't understand it. I always will. And there's nothing left now but for you to take me home, and for me to try to forget him.'

Ida held her close. It was sweet to have her lamb again, and to be able to mother her, fuss over her, befriend her, as she had done in the past. But it broke her heart to see Rosemary like this. Over Rosemary's fair head Ida stared at nothing, and her lips became a thin line.

'No!' she broke out. 'I'm hanged if I'm going to take you home. Not until I've spoken my mind to those two. Why, that nasty treacherous Spanish — !' Ida uttered a word which had possibly never been used in Villa Lucia before. 'If she gives me any of her sauce, I'll chop her in pieces. I'm not having you with a broken heart, and a life wrecked, if *I* can help it.'

Rosemary drew away from her.

'Nothing can be done now.'

'Never say die with me,' was Ida's retort.

'You don't know how I've tried . . . '

'Yes, and you look half dead, you poor lamb. But now Ida's going to take up the cudgels on your behalf.'

'You couldn't do anything. Paul wouldn't listen to you . . . '

'Mark my words, he will!'

'Oh, don't even try. Just let's go home together.'

'If you love that man, he's going to

do something about it,' said Ida doggedly.

But Rosemary continued to reiterate: 'It's too late . . . too late!'

* * *

That night Ida Bryant dined up in Rosemary's bedroom with her friend. Ida insisted upon Rosemary returning to her bed.

'You look too darn poorly for words, and I'm going to see that you get some rest,' she said.

'You're a darling, Ida,' Rosemary had replied, and obeyed without protest.

But, later in the evening, Ida took it upon herself to go downstairs. She both felt and looked a trifle pompous in the one and only evening dress which she had brought out with her. Blue lace over pink georgette. It hung badly, and looked awful. But Ida held her head high, and her bosom swelled with virtuous indignation as she walked down the marble staircase. She was going to see Rosemary's husband, in spite of all that poor little Romie had to say, and that was that!

At the foot of the stairs she met a girl coming out of the library. A fair, strikingly handsome young woman in black, with a white rose, Spanish-wise, behind one ear. Ida immediately jumped to conclusions. This must be Mercedes Lamanda, or Cadozza, or whatever she called herself. At any rate she was the person responsible for poor little Romie's troubles. Ida pursed her lips and advanced upon the Spaniard.

'Here!' she said, half closing an eye. 'Is your name Mercydees?'

Mercedes stopped and looked at her with some astonishment. Heavens, she thought, what a sight! And this was the English Señorita, the *amiga* of Rose-Marie! Mercedes put a hand on one hip and eyed her a trifle scornfully.

'That is my name,' she said, in her broken English.

'Then here's where I tell you what I

think of you,' said Ida, her indignation swelling. And for the next five minutes she spoke without taking breath. She said precisely what she thought. She poured good solid, British abuse upon the Spanish beauty which left Mercedes white and gasping. Half of the insults she did not understand, but many of them were made plain to her and, it was certainly plain enough that Miss Bryant was accusing her of having instigated the whole trouble.

When Ida paused for breath, Mercedes said something equally passionate in Spanish, snapped her fingers, and tried to pass Ida on the staircase, but Ida, with arms outstretched, barred her way.

'No, you don't, you nasty little cat! You're not getting by me until I've had your promise that you'll leave Rosemary and her husband alone and get out of the house.'

Mercedes' black eyes sparkled with rage.

'How dare you, you ugly old woman!'

she said, and turned to go the other way.

Then Ida's large and bony hand caught her shoulder. Mercedes gave a little cry of pain.

'*Dios*; how dare you lay hands on me! Let me go.'

'Not until you promise . . . '

Mercedes, suddenly frightened, for she was a coward, screamed aloud:

'*Ola! Pablo! Pablo!*'

Don Pablo heard that cry, and emerged from the library, where he was sitting trying to concentrate upon some correspondence. He hastened into the hall, and for a moment was bewildered by the sight of the gaunt female in her blue and pink draperies, standing like a statue of wrath on the wide staircase, clutching Mercedes' arm.

'What on earth is this?' he asked.

Mercedes screamed shrilly in Spanish:

'This is the English friend of your charming wife, and she is mad. She is trying to bully me.'

Before Paul could answer, Ida Bryant released Mercedes, and advanced with equal courage upon Don Pablo. With some scorn she looked at the handsome figure in the faultless evening clothes.

'Excuse me, Don Pablo, but I am not standing for any nonsense either from you or this girl, Mercedes. Talk about bullying! You have both bullied my little pal upstairs until she's a nervous wreck, and, now I'm here, it's got to stop. You're just making the biggest mistake of your life, Mr. Don Pablo, and you're going to hear about it from me, and I don't care what you say!'

'She's a lunatic!' Mercedes muttered.

Paul raised one ironic eyebrow, and his lips curved into that freezing smile which Rosemary, had she seen it would have taken as a warning. But it had no effect upon Ida.

'You're going to listen to me for a few minutes, young fella me lad,' she said.

Paul had probably never in his life been addressed in such a fashion. Suddenly he burst out laughing.

'I find this comic,' he exclaimed.

'Well, I don't,' said Mercedes sullenly.

'You shut up!' Ida turned on her. 'I should think that poor girl upstairs has had about enough of you and your interference. Now you leave me to have my say.'

Don Pablo ceased laughing.

'I don't think, Miss Bryant, that it will be of much avail if you 'have your say,' as you call it.'

'But you're going to listen to me.'

'Am I?'

'Yes,' said Ida. 'And you'll get no peace from me until you've listened.'

'Then pray come into the library and get it over,' he said. 'For the one thing I most desire is peace.'

'Don't listen to her, Pablo,' said Mercedes.

'Well, if you listen to *that* little reptile, you'll get about as much peace as you'd find in an asylum,' was Ida's comment. 'If you don't mind me saying so, Mr. Don Pablo, you're a fool if you've allowed that slimy little brute to talk you over instead of believing what my pal had to say to you.'

Paul, irritated, and yet half amused by this extraordinary product of the British Isles, shrugged his shoulders, opened the library door, and bade her enter.

Mercedes was left outside, chewing her handkerchief in fury. The last thing she wanted was for Rosemary's friend to influence Pablo in any way. But, since Paul was willing to listen to her, what was to be done about it?

In the library Paul listened for a good half hour, and he was not allowed to do much talking, because Ida on the war path was a passionate and courageous fighter. She was fighting now for her 'lamb,' and she wasn't going to allow any Spaniard, English-educated or otherwise, to frighten *her*.

She told Paul what she thought of him. He was a cad, a brute, a blackguard, to have taken advantage of the silly joke Rosemary had played upon him in the first place, and kept her here. And, once having lived with her as his wife, he was everything that was bad for not treating her better. He must realise, she said, that Rosemary was a mere child, and that there was nothing whatsoever of the scheming adventuress about her. Hadn't he the sense to realise that that sly Spanish creature, Mercydees, was at the root of all the trouble, and possibly his cousin too, from what Ida had heard? Why should he believe all that Mercydees had to say and not Rosemary?

One question after another Ida hurled at Paul, who listened, smoking in silence, not a muscle of his face moving. Then, when he was allowed to speak, he reminded Miss Bryant, with chilly sarcasm, that he had ample proof of his wife's infamous conduct. He had tried to believe in her — had wanted to. He had even overlooked the poisoning episode. He was prepared to believe that he had other enemies beside herself. But what of the letter she had received? Had Rosemary told Miss Bryant about that?

'Yes, she told me about that,' said Ida.

And it was never really written to her, she said. It was just another link that those two scheming wretches were trying to put in the chain of evidence that they had forged against Rosemary.

Paul began to walk up and down the library. He felt restless and nervous — and all that Miss Bryant was saying stirred up the old violent longing to believe in Rose-Marie. He could not kill his deep-rooted passion for her. He wanted to. He wanted to put her right out of his mind and his life. He had decided to leave Villa Lucia to-morrow and never see his wife again. Why had he ever allowed this ridiculous, unattractive spinster, who called herself Rose-Marie's best friend, to come and trouble his mind and set him wondering, doubting, again?

'You're a cruel monster, the way you've treated her,' Miss Bryant hurled at him. 'If you could only see her . . . thoroughly done-in . . . you and that Spanish girl between you have half killed her! And when I asked her why she had put up with so much, what did she answer? 'Because I loved him,' she said . . . with tears all running down her cheeks. Poor lamb! As if anybody who knew her could suspect her of all this villainy! You're not such a clever gentleman as you look, Mr. Don Pablo.'

Paul swung round, shaking, his forehead damp, his dark eyes wild and bright.

'I won't believe you! I don't see why I should! I've had enough proof . . . '

'Bah!' Ida Bryant interrupted. 'You don't know where you're being duped . . . you're turning an ear to the wrong crowd. And I tell you, if you let that poor child leave Spain in the condition of mind that she's in now, you'll have it on your conscience for the rest of your life. *I* wouldn't like to be in your shoes!'

He looked at her speechlessly. He

didn't know why he was standing all this abuse, all these accusations, from this woman. He had only to ring and call his servants and he could have her turned out of the *hacienda*, and yet, something fine and fearless in the plain, homely creature who was a typist from London, made him bow, mentally, before her, in spite of himself. He knew there was no intrigue about this woman, nothing false or treacherous. She was straight as a die. She believed in Rose-Marie. Rose-Marie was upstairs, ill and weeping . . . declaring her love for him. That was queer! Why hadn't she rushed to Harry's arms, which was what Mercedes led him to believe she would do. *Madre de Dios*, but he would go out of his mind if he could not get this terrible business straightened out for good and all.

He would listen to no more from Ida Bryant.

'I've had enough,' he told her. 'I'm far from fit myself. I'm going to my room. To-morrow I will see . . . my wife

. . . and talk to her.'

Ida drew a deep breath. Now that the scene was over she was on the verge of tears.

'Well, I'm glad you've got that much sense,' she said. 'Good night.'

He bowed.

'Good night.'

'And have you no message for Romie?'

A spasm crossed Don Pablo's features.

He seemed in an instant to see Rose-Marie standing before him in her white velvet dress with the diamond cross glittering on her breast. Rose-Marie, the fair, the chaste, melting to passion only in his arms. And he wanted, madly, to believe in all that Ida Bryant had told him to-night.

'No message,' he said hoarsely. 'But I'll see her . . . to-morrow.'

And that was all that Ida Bryant could tell Rosemary when she returned to her friend's bedroom. Rosemary, lying on her pillows like a languid lily, clung to Ida's hands, but remained uncomforted.

'It doesn't mean anything . . . Paul just saying that he'll see me. He'll only hurl all those hateful accusations at me again. I can't prove myself innocent if he chooses to believe the others. You shouldn't have bothered, Ida darling, but I thank you, with all my heart.'

Ida kissed her, and tucked her up as though she were a baby.

'Don't be too downhearted, my lamb. Something tells me that everything will come right in the end. And I may as well tell you that I don't think that husband of yours is too bad. When he dropped all that icy-Don-Pablo-business he became quite human, and I bet he's still in love with you, whatever he says.'

For the next few hours, alone in her darkened bedroom, Rosemary tried to console herself with those words. But, every time she thought of Paul, she dissolved into tears, and told herself, broken-heartedly, that he hated her. Ida was wrong. He was no longer in love with her, and never would be again.

It was in the early hours of the morning, when that heavy darkness immediately before the dawn was still shrouding Villa Lucia, that Rosemary fell into a troubled sleep.

She awakened with a violent start to see the shutters of her balcony opening. Very slowly they moved apart. For an instant Rosemary stared at the dark figure of a man which moved quickly into her room. Fear held her transfixed. At first she thought this was a mountain robber . . . a daring gipsy . . . a cut-throat of some sort, in search of her jewels. Then the man spoke:

'Rosemary!'

The violent beating of her heart died somewhat. She picked up a little velvet wrap and covered her bare shoulders.

'Good God . . . you, Harry Dyall!'

He bent over the bed.

'Yes. I've come to take you away, Rose-Marie. Mercedes sent for me. She said that you intended leaving the villa in the morning. You don't want to go with your friend. You want to come with me. I am the one who will take care of you.'

She shrank away. She could not see his face very well, but she could smell his breath. It reeked of alcohol. He had been drinking, and he was not sane. Of that she was sure.

'Go away,' she said. 'Go on . . . quickly, or I'll call for my friend, who is in the next room.'

He made a savage lunge at her, and caught her arms.

'Damn your friend. You're going to listen to me . . .'

'I'll give you one more chance. Either you get out, or I'll scream.'

'You don't dare. Paul thinks I'm your lover, and if I'm found here with you I shall tell him that you sent for me.'

Only for an instant was she frightened by this. Then, when she felt his hot face against hers, she lost control and screamed.

'Paul! Paul!'

Yes, it was for Paul whom she called, and not Ida. It was Paul she wanted, and it was Paul who came.

Don Pablo was not asleep. He had been awake most of the night, and the reading-lamp was still alight beside his bed. Hour after hour he smoked and brooded, trying to make up his mind what to do, what to say, when he next saw his wife.

When he heard Rosemary's frenzied voice, he flung on a dressing-gown and rushed to her room. Mercedes, also awakened, made an appearance on the landing, and followed to the scene of action.

Don Pablo caught the sound of Rosemary's voice as he opened the door.

'Let me go. Paul will kill you if he finds you here. You won't get the best of it, this time. I'm absolutely innocent, and I won't be blamed . . . I won't . . . I won't!'

'Great God!' Paul thought. 'Harry is in there.'

Harry, in Rose-Marie's bedroom . . . and she had called for him, her husband. She did not want Harry. She was absolutely innocent. She was telling Harry so.

Paul burst into the room.

'Rose-Marie! . . . where are you? Harry . . . you swine . . . '

He could see nothing. The room was in darkness. He moved forward, fumbling for the light.

But the next moment a shot was fired. Harry Dyall, mad with drink, had pulled a revolver from his coat pocket and fired blindly, in the direction of Paul's voice.

Rosemary screamed!

'Paul . . . Paul!'

And then there was a deep, sighing moan, and, after that, silence.

The lights flashed on. It was Ida Bryant who found the switch. Rosemary, sitting up in bed, wide-eyed with horror, stared around her. The first thing she saw was the figure of Paul, standing there, tall and straight, in the centre of the room. She gave a sobbing cry.

'Then he didn't get you! Oh, thank God!'

'No,' said Paul slowly. '*But whom did he hit?*'

Then they all turned, and saw on the floor, in the doorway, the body of a girl in a black satin wrapper. Mercedes, like a grotesque doll, sprawling there motionless, her fair head dabbled in blood.

'The bullet got *her*,' Paul said hoarsely. 'She was just behind me.'

'Oh!' said Rosemary, 'oh,' and turned and buried her face in the pillow, shuddering from head to foot.

Ida Bryant hurried to her, and took her in her arms as though to shield her from the horror.

But Paul knelt beside the body of the Spanish girl . . . not yet a lifeless corpse, although she was fast dying when he lifted her up. Her great black eyes stared up at him.

'*Santa Maria*, pray for me . . . I am

finished . . . it was an act of God . . . the bullet meant for you . . . to kill *me* . . . what an irony!'

'Hush, we will get a doctor for you, and you will be all right.'

'No, I am dying, and I cannot go with this sin on my soul. Rose-Marie . . . is innocent. It is all my fault . . . and Harry's.'

Paul stared over her head. He was too bewildered to think. The main thing that he felt was a growing frenzy of longing to get at Harry . . . Harry who had vanished out of that window and got away before the lights went up.

Mercedes made her confession . . . gasped it with her last breath, and died there in his arms, clinging to the crucifix which a servant had given him, and which he had pressed between her hands.

And then all thoughts cleared from Paul's brain save one . . . the knowledge that his wife was guiltless, and that the whole ugly sinister plot had been cleared up at last. Mercedes had sinned, and had paid for her sins with death. Harry had sinned, and he was going to pay. But none of that mattered. It was only Rose-Marie's innocence that mattered.

Don Pablo found himself alone in his wife's bedroom. The servants were carrying what had been Mercedes Cadozza to her room. A doctor had been called for. The villa was alight and alive with people hurrying to and fro. And Ida Bryant, ever discreet, had slipped quietly away to her own room.

Rosemary, her face white and wet with tears, looked speechlessly at her husband. And he, equally unable to speak, knelt down beside her and laid his head upon her breast. Immediately her arms went round him. The feeling of horror was chased from her brain. She whispered:

'Paul, darling . . . you didn't know . . . Paul, it wasn't your fault, don't blame yourself . . . nothing matters now, except that you *know*, and it's going to be all right.'

His arms enfolded her, but still he could not speak. But she felt his hot tears soaking through the thin chiffon of her nightgown ... burning and eloquent of his desire to be forgiven ... a desire which she, woman-like, was so ready to fulfil.

★ ★ ★

Perhaps it took many long months before either Paul or Rosemary could forget that sinister night when Mercedes died from the effects of the bullet which had been meant for Paul. But in time the unhappy memory of that, and of all the dark weeks preceding it, faded.

Harry Dyall did not live to take his trial for the manslaughter of Mercedes, neither did he receive the punishment which Paul might personally have given him. On that same black night he fired another shot, and ended his own wasted life. Two *guardia civil* found him in a deserted part of the Malaga road, dead, in his car, a bullet wound through his brain.

And so Don Pablo and his wife walked hand in hand from the shadows into the light.

Ida Bryant did not return quite as early as was anticipated to England. And, once affairs were happily settled for her 'lamb,' she began to discover that Spain was really quite an attractive place, and that all Spaniards were neither barbaric nor dangerous. In fact she even began to like them, and to appreciate the Andalusian country which meant so much sunlight, fruit, flowers, song, laughter!

It brought her intense happiness to see Rosemary looking so well and happy. It did not take long before the colour came back to her cheeks and the shining light into her eyes. Paul loved her. He was never tired of telling her so, or of begging her to forgive him for all that he had made her suffer in the past.

And when Ida Bryant took that train journey back to England, Paul and

Rosemary went with her. Paul had marvellous plans for the future. He fully shared his wife's affection for the homely Ida, and, although she would not admit it, she secretly adored him. One of his first actions was to make her independent and buy her a little poultry farm, which was *her* idea of heaven, near the Sussex Downs.

And once Ida was settled, Paul and Rosemary travelled out to Spain again. Neither of them had any wish to return to Villa Lucia. There were too many unhappy memories clinging to it still. So Paul sold it, and bought another equally beautiful place for his young wife, not far from the village of Torremolinos, facing the sea.

And it was there that Rosemary's son was born. That son which Harry Dyall had hoped she would never bear, and who would inherit his father's title and estates. Both Paul and Rosemary had longed for a child, although Paul had been terrified of the consequences so far as his wife was concerned. He could not bear that his lovely Rose-Marie should suffer one instant's pain. But Rosemary was young and strong, and, as she told him, the pain was so soon forgotten.

Her son was glorious. He set the seal on her happiness. He had her fair silky head, and his father's dark expressive eyes and finely shaped hands.

'He is perfect,' Rosemary told her husband when the nurses left her alone with Paul on the day that the baby was born.

Don Pablo, sitting beside her, looked at her . . . and worshipped. Rose-Marie, lovely and glowing like a rose, with her son in her arms . . . what a picture for a poet or artist to rave about, he thought emotionally.

'*You* are perfect,' he said.

'What shall we call him?' she asked dreamily.

'Anything you like.'

'Then, 'Pablo' it must be, after you.'

'But he must be a better man than I have been, Rose-Marie.'

'That would be impossible.'

'He must be like his exquisite mother.'

'No, much, much better than I am!'

'That I assure you, would be impossible.'

Their eyes met, and they both laughed happily, confident of each other's love.

And then the young heir to the Iballos, although but a few hours old, decided that he was of importance in this world and must not be left out. His young and beautiful mother and his handsome father were engrossed in each other. They were excluding him. He cried . . . and was drawn immediately into the circle of their love.

We do hope that you have enjoyed reading this large print book.

Did you know that all of our titles are available for purchase?

We publish a wide range of high quality large print books including:
Romances, Mysteries, Classics
General Fiction
Non Fiction and Westerns

Special interest titles available in large print are:
The Little Oxford Dictionary
Music Book, Song Book
Hymn Book, Service Book

Also available from us courtesy of Oxford University Press:
Young Readers' Dictionary
(large print edition)
Young Readers' Thesaurus
(large print edition)

For further information or a free brochure, please contact us at:
Ulverscroft Large Print Books Ltd.,
The Green, Bradgate Road, Anstey,
Leicester, LE7 7FU, England.
Tel: (00 44) **0116 236 4325**
Fax: (00 44) **0116 234 0205**

WHERE DUTY LIES

Patricia Robins

The minute Charlotte sees Meridan Avebury at a wedding, it causes such a sudden feeling in her heart that she believes it must be love at first sight. But Meridan is already engaged to the beautiful Phillipa, who is dangerously ill. And while they don't deny their feelings for each other, Charlotte and Meridan are unwilling to take their own happiness at Phillipa's expense. However, Meridan becomes troubled by divided loyalties and struggles to find where duty really lies.

SHADOWS OF DANGER

Angela Dracup

Diana is uneasy when she has a premonition of an air disaster. But when she meets charismatic widower Louis, she is terrified — for he is the man in her dream. Soon she is in love with Louis, but her fear for his safety becomes acute. It seems the only way she can protect him is to marry a man she does not love. Would Louis ever forgive her for leaving him? Would true love eventually win through?

TO LOVE AGAIN

Chrissie Loveday

It is 1945 and the lives of families have changed. The pain and memories of the war years have left their mark. Lizzie Vale, the carefree girl — once an aspiring journalist — has changed and become a dedicated nurse. She fights to help her patients recover from their terrible injuries and falls in love with Daniel Miles. Could they ever have a future? Injuries and family prejudice present seemingly insuperable obstacles, but Lizzie is a force to be reckoned with.